The Gem Collector

P. G. WODEHOUSE

The Gem Collector

P. G. Wodehouse

© 1st World Library, 2006
PO Box 2211
Fairfield, IA 52556
www.1stworldlibrary.com
First Edition

LCCN: 2006938097

Softcover ISBN: 978-1-4218-3396-5
Hardcover ISBN: 978-1-4218-3296-8
eBook ISBN: 978-1-4218-3496-2

Purchase *"The Gem Collector"*
as a traditional bound book at:
www.1stWorldLibrary.com/purchase.asp?ISBN=978-1-4218-3396-5

1st World Library is a literary, educational organization
dedicated to:

- Creating a free internet library of downloadable ebooks

  - Hosting writing competitions and offering book
    publishing scholarships.

Interested in more 1st World Library books?
contact: literacy@1stworldlibrary.com
Check us out at: www.1stworldlibrary.com

1st World Library Literary Society

Giving Back to the World

"If you want to work on the core problem, it's early school literacy."
- James Barksdale, former CEO of Netscape

"No skill is more crucial to the future of a child, or to a democratic and prosperous society, than literacy."

- Los Angeles Times

Literacy... means far more than learning how to read and write... The aim is to transmit... knowledge and promote social participation."

- UNESCO

"Literacy is not a luxury, it is a right and a responsibility. If our world is to meet the challenges of the twenty-first century we must harness the energy and creativity of all our citizens."

- President Bill Clinton

"Parents should be encouraged to read to their children, and teachers should be equipped with all available techniques for teaching literacy, so the varying needs and capacities of individual kids can be taken into account."

- Hugh Mackay

CHAPTER I

The supper room of the Savoy Hotel was all brightness and glitter and gayety. But Sir James Willoughby Pitt, baronet, of the United Kingdom, looked round about him through the smoke of his cigarette, and felt moodily that this was a flat world, despite the geographers, and that he was very much alone in it.

He felt old.

If it is ever allowable for a young man of twenty-six to give himself up to melancholy reflections, Jimmy Pitt might have been excused for doing so, at that moment. Nine years ago he had dropped out, or, to put it more exactly, had been kicked out, and had ceased to belong to London. And now he had returned to find himself in a strange city.

Jimmy Pitt's complete history would take long to write, for he had contrived to crowd much into those nine years. Abridged, it may be told as follows: There were two brothers, a good brother and a bad brother. Sir Eustace Pitt, the latter, married money. John, his younger brother, remained a bachelor. It may be mentioned, to check needless sympathy, that there was no rivalry between the two. John Pitt had not the slightest desire to marry the lady of his brother's choice, or any other lady. He was a self-sufficing man who from an early age showed signs of becoming some day a financial magnate.

Matters went on much the same after the marriage. John

continued to go to the city, Eustace to the dogs. Neither brother had any money of his own, the fortune of the Pitts having been squandered to the ultimate farthing by the portive gentleman who had held the title in the days of the regency, when White's and the Cocoa Tree were in their prime, and fortunes had a habit of disappearing in a single evening. Four years after the marriage, Lady Pitt died, and the widower, having spent three years and a half at Monte Carlo, working out an infallible system for breaking the bank, to the great contentment of Mons. Blanc and the management in general, proceeded to the gardens, where he shot himself in the orthodox manner, leaving many liabilities, few assets, and one son.

The good brother, by this time a man of substance in Lombard Street, adopted the youthful successor to the title, and sent him to a series of schools, beginning with a kindergarten and ending with Eton.

Unfortunately Eton demanded from Jimmy a higher standard of conduct than he was prepared to supply, and a week after his seventeenth birthday, his career as an Etonian closed prematurely. John Pitt thereupon delivered an ultimatum. Jimmy could choose between the smallest of small posts in his uncle's business, and one hundred pounds in banknotes, coupled with the usual handwashing and disowning. Jimmy would not have been his father's son if he had not dropped at the money. The world seemed full to him of possibilities for a young man of parts with a hundred pounds in his pocket.

He left for Liverpool that day, and for New York on the morrow.

For the next nine years he is off the stage, which is occupied by his Uncle John, proceeding from strength to strength, now head partner, next chairman of the company into which the business had been converted, and finally a member of Parliament, silent as a wax figure, but a great comfort to the party by virtue of liberal contributions to its funds.

It may be thought curious that he should make Jimmy his heir after what had happened; but it is possible that time had softened his resentment. Or he may have had a dislike for public charities, the only other claimant for his wealth. At any rate, it came about that Jimmy, reading in a Chicago paper that if Sir James Willoughby Pitt, baronet, would call upon Messrs. Snell, Hazlewood, and Delane, solicitors, of Lincoln's Inn Fields, London, he would hear of something to his advantage, had called and heard something very much to his advantage.

Wherefore we find him, on this night of July, supping in lonely magnificence at the Savoy, and feeling at the moment far less conscious of the magnificence than of the loneliness.

Watching the crowd with a jaundiced eye, Jimmy had found his attention attracted chiefly by a party of three a few tables away. The party consisted of a pretty girl, a lady of middle age and stately demeanor, plainly her mother, and a light-haired, weedy young man of about twenty. It had been the almost incessant prattle of this youth and the peculiarly high-pitched, gurgling laugh which shot from him at short intervals which had drawn Jimmy's notice upon them. And it was the curious cessation of both prattle and laugh which now made him look again in their direction.

The young man faced Jimmy; and Jimmy, looking at him, could see that all was not well with him. He was pale. He talked at random. A slight perspiration was noticeable on his forehead.

Jimmy caught his eye. There was a hunted look in it.

Given the time and the place, there were only two things which could have caused that look. Either the light-haired young man had seen a ghost, or he had suddenly realized that he had not enough money to pay the check.

Jimmy's heart went out to the sufferer. He took a card from

his case, scribbled the words, "Can I help?" on it, and gave it to waiter to take to the young man, who was now in a state bordering on collapse.

The next moment the light-haired one was at his table, talking in a feverish whisper.

"I say," he said, "it's frightfully good of you, old chap. It's frightfully awkward. I've come out with too little money. I hardly like to—What I mean to say is, you've never seen me before, and—"

"That's all right," said Jimmy. "Only too glad to help. It might have happened to any one. Will this be enough?"

He placed a five-pound note on the table. The young man grabbed at it with a rush of thanks.

"I say, thanks fearfully," he said. "I don't know what I'd have done. I'll let you have it back to-morrow. Here's my card. Blunt's my name. Spennie Blunt. Is your address on your card? I can't remember. Oh, by Jove, I've got it in my hand all the time." The gurgling laugh came into action again, freshened and strengthened by its rest. "Savoy Mansions, eh? I'll come round to-morrow. Thanks, frightfully, again old chap. I don't know what I should have done."

He flitted back to his table, bearing the spoil, and Jimmy, having finished his cigarette, paid his check, and got up to go.

It was a perfect summer night. He looked at his watch. There was time for a stroll on the Embankment before bed.

He was leaning on the balustrade, looking across the river at the vague, mysterious mass of buildings on the Surrey side, when a voice broke in on his thoughts.

"Say, boss. Excuse me."

P. G. Wodehouse

Jimmy spun round. A ragged man with a crop of fiery red hair was standing at his side. The light was dim, but Jimmy recognized that hair.

"Spike!" he cried.

The other gaped, then grinned a vast grin of recognition.

"Mr. Chames! Gee, dis cops de limit!"

Three years had passed since Jimmy had parted from Spike Mullins, Red Spike to the New York police, but time had not touched him. To Jimmy he looked precisely the same as in the old New York days.

A policeman sauntered past, and glanced curiously at them. He made as if to stop, then walked on. A few yards away he halted. Jimmy could see him watching covertly. He realized that this was not the place for a prolonged conversation.

"Spike," he said, "do you know Savoy Mansions?"

"Sure. Foist to de left across de way."

"Come on there. I'll meet you at the door. We can't talk here. That cop's got his eye on us."

He walked away. As he went, he smiled. The policeman's inspection had made him suddenly alert and on his guard. Yet why? What did it matter to Sir James Pitt, baronet, if the whole police force of London stopped and looked at him?

"Queer thing, habit," he said, as he made his way across the road.

CHAPTER II

A black figure detached itself from the blacker shadows, and shuffled stealthily to where Jimmy stood on the doorstep.

"That you, Spike?" asked Jimmy, in a low voice.

"Dat's right, Mr. Chames."

"Come on in."

He led the way up to his rooms, switched on the electric light, and shut the door. Spike stood blinking at the sudden glare. He twirled his battered hat in his hands. His red hair shone fiercely.

Jimmy inspected him out of the corner of his eye, and came to the conclusion that the Mullins finances must be at a low ebb. Spike's costume differed in several important details from that of the ordinary well-groomed man about town. There was nothing of the *flaneur* about the Bowery boy. His hat was of the soft black felt, fashionable on the East Side of New York. It was in poor condition, and looked as if it had been up too late the night before. A black tail coat, burst at the elbows, stained with mud, was tightly buttoned across his chest. This evidently with the idea of concealing the fact that he wore no shirt—an attempt which was not wholly successful. A pair of gray flannel trousers and boots out of which two toes peeped coyly, completed the picture.

P. G. Wodehouse

Even Spike himself seemed to be aware that there were points in his appearance which would have distressed the editor of a men's fashion paper.

"'Scuse dese duds," he said. "Me man's bin an' mislaid de trunk wit' me best suit in. Dis is me number two."

"Don't mention it, Spike," said Jimmy. "You look like a matinee idol. Have a drink?"

Spike's eye gleamed as he reached for the decanter. He took a seat.

"Cigar, Spike?"

"Sure. T'anks, Mr. Chames."

Jimmy lit his pipe. Spike, after a few genteel sips, threw off his restraint and finished the rest of his glass at a gulp.

"Try another," suggested Jimmy.

Spike's grin showed that the idea had been well received.

Jimmy sat and smoked in silence for a while. He was thinking the thing over. He had met Spike Mullins for the first time in rather curious circumstances in New York, and for four years the other had followed him with a fidelity which no dangers or hardships could affect. Whatever "Mr. Chames" did, said, or thought was to Spike the best possible act, speech, or reflection of which man was capable. For four years their partnership had continued, and then, conducting a little adventure on his own account in Jimmy's absence, Spike had met with one of those accidents which may happen to any one. The police had gathered him in, and he had passed out of Jimmy's life.

What was puzzling Jimmy was the problem of what to do with him now that he had reentered it. Mr. Chames was one man. Sir James Willoughby Pitt, baronet, another. On the other hand, Spike was plainly in low water, and must be lent a helping hand.

Spike was looking at him over his glass with respectful admiration. Jimmy caught his eye, and spoke.

"Well, Spike," he said. "Curious, us meeting like this."

"De limit," agreed Spike.

"I can't imagine you three thousand miles away from New York. How do you know the cars still run both ways on Broadway?"

A wistful look came into Spike's eye.

"I t'ought it was time I give old Lunnon a call. De cops seemed like as if they didn't have no use for me in New York. Dey don't give de glad smile to a boy out of prison."

"Poor old Spike," said Jimmy, "you've had bad luck, haven't you?"

"Fierce," agreed the other.

"But whatever induced you to try for that safe without me? They were bound to get you. You should have waited."

"Dat's right, boss, if I never says anudder word. I was a farmer for fair at de game wit'out youse. But I t'ought I'd try to do somet'ing so dat I'd have somet'ing to show youse when you come back. So I says here's dis safe and here's me, and I'll get busy wit' it, and den Mr. Chames will be pleased for fair when he gets back. So I has a try, and dey gets me while I'm at it. We'll cut out dat part."

"Well, it's over now, at any rate. What have you been doing since you came to England?"

"Gettin' moved on by de cops, mostly. An' sleepin' in de park."

"Well, you needn't sleep in the park any more, Spike. You can pitch your moving tent with me. And you'll want some clothes. We'll get those to-morrow. You're the sort of figure they can fit off the peg. You're not too tall, which is a good thing."

"Bad t'ing for me, Mr. Chames. If I'd bin taller I'd have stood for being a New York cop, and bin buying a brownstone house on Fifth Avenue by this. It's de cops makes de big money in old Manhattan, dat's who it is."

"You're right there," said Jimmy. "At least, partly. I suppose half the New York force does get rich by graft. There are honest men among them, but we didn't happen to meet them."

"That's right, we didn't. Dere was old man McEachern."

"McEachern! Yes. If any of them got rich, he would be the man. He was the worst grafter of the entire bunch. I could tell you some stories about old Pat McEachern, Spike. If half those yarns were true he must be a wealthy man by now. We shall hear of him running for mayor one of these days."

"Say, Mr. Chames, wasn't youse struck on de goil?"

"What girl?" said Jimmy quietly.

"Old man McEachern's goil, Molly. Dey used to say dat youse was her steady."

"If you don't mind, Spike, friend of my youth, we'll cut out that," said Jimmy. "When I want my affairs discussed I'll mention it. Till then—See?"

"Sure," said Spike, who saw nothing beyond the fact, dimly

realized, that he had said something which had been better left unsaid.

Jimmy chewed the stem of his pipe savagely. Spike's words seemed to have touched a spring and let loose feelings which he had kept down for three years. Molly McEachern! So "they" used to say that he was engaged to Molly. He cursed Spike Mullins in his heart, well-meaning, blundering Spike, who was now sitting on the edge of his chair drawing sorrowfully at his cigar and wondering what he had done to give offense. The years fell away from Jimmy, and he was back in New York, standing at the corner of Forty-second Street with half an hour to wait because the fear of missing her had sent him there too early; sitting in Central Park with her while the squirrels came down and begged for nuts; walking—Damn Spike! They had been friends. Nothing more. He had never said a word. Her father had warned her against him. Old Pat McEachern knew how he got his living, and could have put his hand on the author of half a dozen burglaries by which the police had been officially "baffled". That had been his strong point. He had never left tracks. There was never any evidence. But McEachern knew, and he had intervened stormily when he came upon them together. And Molly had stood up for him, till her father had apologized confusedly, raging inwardly the while at his helplessness. It was after that—

"Mr. Chames," said Spike.

Jimmy's wits returned.

"Hullo?" he said.

"Mr. Chames, what's doing here? Put me next to de game. Is it de old lay? You'll want me wit' youse, I guess?"

Jimmy laughed, and shut the door on his dreams.

"I'd quite forgotten I hadn't told you about myself, Spike. Do you know what a baronet is?"

"Search me. What's de answer?"

"A baronet's the noblest work of man, Spike. I am one. Let wealth and commerce, laws and learning—or is it art and learning?—die, but leave us still our old nobility. I'm a big man now, Spike, I can tell you."

"Gee!"

"My position has also the advantage of carrying a good deal of money with it."

"Plunks!"

"You have grasped it. Plunks. Dollars. Doubloons. I line up with the thickwads now, Spike. I don't have to work to turn a dishonest penny any longer."

The horrid truth sank slowly into the other's mind.

"Say! What, Mr. Chames? Youse don't need to go on de old lay no more? You're cutting it out for fair?"

"That's the idea."

Spike gasped. His world was falling about his ears. Now that he had met Mr. Chames again he had looked forward to a long and prosperous partnership in crime, with always the master mind behind him to direct his movements and check him if he went wrong. He had looked out upon the richness of London, and he had said with Bluecher: "What a city to loot!"

And here was his leader shattering his visions with a word.

"Have another drink, Spike," said the lost leader sympathetically. "It's a shock to you, I guess."

"I t'ought, Mr. Chames—"

"I know you did, and I'm very sorry for you. But it can't be helped. *Noblesse oblige*, Spike. We of the old aristocracy mustn't do these things. We should get ourselves talked about."

Spike sat silent, with a long face. Jimmy slapped him on the shoulder.

"After all," he said, "living honestly may be the limit, for all we know. Numbers of people do it, I've heard, and enjoy themselves tremendously. We must give it a trial, Spike. We'll go out together and see life. Pull yourself together and be cheerful, Spike."

After a moment's reflection the other grinned, howbeit faintly.

"That's right," said Jimmy Pitt. "You'll be the greatest success ever in society. All you have to do is to brush your hair, look cheerful, and keep your hands off the spoons. For in society, Spike, they invariably count them after the departure of the last guest."

"Sure," said Spike, as one who thoroughly understood this sensible precaution.

"And now," said Jimmy, "we'll be turning in. Can you manage sleeping on the sofa for one night?"

"Gee, I've bin sleepin' on de Embankment all de last week. Dis is to de good, Mister Chames."

CHAPTER III

In the days before the Welshman began to expend his surplus energy in playing football, he was accustomed, whenever the monotony of his everyday life began to oppress him, to collect a few friends and make raids across the border into England, to the huge discomfort of the dwellers on the other side. It was to cope with this habit that Corven Abbey, in Shropshire, came into existence. It met a long-felt want. Ministering to the spiritual needs of the neighborhood in times of peace, it became a haven of refuge when trouble began. From all sides people poured into it, emerging cautiously when the marauders had disappeared.

In the whole history of the abbey there is but one instance recorded of a bandit attempting to take the place by storm, and the attack was an emphatic failure. On receipt of one ladle full of molten lead, aimed to a nicety by John the Novice, who seems to have been anything but a novice at marksmanship, this warrior retired, done to a turn, to his mountain fastnesses, and is never heard of again. He would seem, however, to have passed the word round among his friends, for subsequent raiding parties studiously avoided the abbey, and a peasant who had succeeded in crossing its threshold was for the future considered to be "home" and out of the game. Corven Abbey, as a result, grew in power and popularity. Abbot succeeded abbot, the lake at the foot of the hill was restocked at intervals, the lichen grew on the walls; and still the abbey endured.

But time, assisted by his majesty, King Henry the Eighth, had done its work. The monks had fled. The walls had crumbled, and in the twentieth century, the abbey was a modern country house, and the owner a rich American.

Of this gentleman the world knew but little. That he had made money, and a good deal of it, was certain. His name, Patrick McEachern, suggested Irish parentage, and a slight brogue, noticeable, however, only in moments of excitement, supported this theory. He had arrived in London some four years back, taken rooms at the Albany, and gone into society.

England still firmly believes that wealth accrues to every resident of New York by some mysterious process not understandable of the Briton. McEachern and his money were accepted by society without question. His solecisms, which at first were numerous, were passed over as so quaint and refreshing. People liked his rugged good humor. He speedily made friends, among them Lady Jane Blunt, the still youthful widow of a man about town, who, after trying for several years to live at the rate of ten thousand per annum with an income of two and a half, had finally given up the struggle and drank himself peacefully into the tomb, leaving her in sole charge of their one son, Spencer Archbald.

Possibly because he was the exact antithesis of the late lamented, Lady Jane found herself drawn to Mr. McEachern. Whatever his faults, he had strength; and after her experience of married life with a weak man, Lady Jane had come to the conclusion that strength was the only male quality worth consideration. When a year later, McEachern's daughter, Molly, had come over, it was Lady Jane who took her under her wing and introduced her everywhere.

In the fifth month of the second year of their acquaintance, Mr. McEachern proposed and was accepted. "The bridegroom," said a society paper, "is one of those typical captains of industry of whom our cousins 'across the streak' can boast so many. Tall, muscular, square-shouldered, with the bulldog jaw and twinkling gray eye of the born leader. You look at

P. G. Wodehouse

him and turn away satisfied. You have seen a man!"

Lady Jane, who had fallen in love with the abbey some years before, during a visit to the neighborhood, had prevailed upon her square-shouldered lord to turn his twinkling gray eye in that direction, and the captain of industry, with the remark that here, at last, was a real bully old sure-fire English stately home, had sent down builders and their like, not in single spies, but in battalions, with instructions to get busy.

The results were excellent. A happy combination of deep purse on the part of the employer and excellent taste on the part of the architect had led to the erection of one of the handsomest buildings in Shropshire. To stand on the hill at the back of the house was to see a view worth remembering. The lower portion of the hill, between the house and the lake, had been cut into broad terraces. The lake itself, with its island with the little boathouse in the centre, was a glimpse of fairyland. Mr. McEachern was not poetical, but he had secured as his private sanctum a room which commanded this view.

He was sitting in this room one evening, about a week after the meeting between Spennie and Jimmy Pitt at the Savoy.

"See, here, Jane," he was saying, "this is my point. I've been fixing up things in my mind, and this is the way I make it out. I reckon there's no sense in taking risks when you needn't. You've a mighty high-toned bunch of guests here. I'm not saying you haven't. What I say is, it would make us all feel more comfortable if we knew there was a detective in the house keeping his eye skinned. I'm not alluding to any of them in particular, but how are we to know that all these social headliners are on the level?"

"If you mean our guests, Pat, I can assure you that they are all perfectly honest."

Lady Jane looked out of the window, as she spoke, at a group of those under discussion. Certainly at the moment the sternest censor could have found nothing to cavil at in their movements. Some were playing tennis, some clock golf, and the rest were smoking. She had frequently complained, in her gentle, languid way, of her husband's unhappily suspicious nature. She could never understand it. For her part she suspected no one. She liked and trusted everybody, which was the reason why she was so popular, and so often taken in.

Mr. McEachern looked bovine, as was his habit when he was endeavoring to gain a point against opposition.

"They may be on the level," he said. "I'm not saying anything against any one. But I've seen a lot of crooks in my time, and it's not the ones with the low brows and the cauliflower ears that you want to watch for. It's the innocent Willies who look as if all they could do was to lead the cotillon and wear bangles on their ankles. I've had a lot to do with them, and it's up to a man that don't want to be stung not to go by what a fellow looks like."

"Really, Pat, dear, I sometimes think you ought to have been a policeman. What *is* the matter?"

"Matter?"

"You shouted."

"Shouted? Not me. Spark from my cigar fell on my hand."

"You know, you smoke too much, Pat," said his wife, seizing the opening with the instinct which makes an Irishman at a fair hit every head he sees.

"I'm all right, me dear. Faith, I c'u'd smoke wan hondred a day and no harm done."

By way of proving the assertion he puffed out with increased vigor at his cigar. The pause gave him time to think of another

P. G. Wodehouse

argument, which might otherwise have escaped him.

"When we were married, me dear Jane," he said, "there was a detective in the room to watch the presents. Two of them. I remimber seeing them at once. There go two of the boys, I said to mysilf. I mean," he added hastily, "two of the police force."

"But detectives at wedding receptions are quite ordinary. Nobody minds them. You see, the presents are so valuable that it would be silly to risk losing them."

"And are there not valuable things here," asked McEachern triumphantly, "which it would be silly to risk losing? And Sir Thomas is coming to-day with his wife. And you know what a deal of jewelry she always takes about her."

"Oh, Julia!" said Lady Jane, a little disdainfully. Her late husband's brother Thomas' wife was one of the few people to whom she objected. And, indeed, she was not alone in this prejudice. Few who had much to do with her did like Lady Blunt.

"That rope of pearls of hers," said Mr. McEachern, "cost forty thousand pounds, no less, so they say."

"So she says. But if you were thinking of bringing down a detective to watch over Julia's necklace, Pat, you needn't trouble. I believe she takes one about with her wherever she goes, disguised as Thomas' valet."

"Still, me dear—"

"Pat, you're absurd," laughed Lady Jane. "I won't have you littering up the house with great, clumsy detectives. You must remember that you aren't in horrid New York now, where everybody you meet wants to rob you. Who is it that you suspect? Who is the—what is the word you're so fond of? Crook. That's it. Who is the crook?"

"I don't want to mention names," said McEachern cautiously, "and I cast no suspicions, but who is that pale, thin Willie who came yesterday? The one that says the clever things that nobody understands?"

"Lulu Wesson! Why, *Pat*rick! He's the most delightful boy. What *can* you suspect him of?"

"I don't suspect him of anything. But you'll remember what I was telling about the sort of boy you want to watch. That's what that boy is. He may be the straightest ever, but if I was told there was a crook in the company, and wasn't put next who it was, he's the boy that would get my vote."

"What dreadful nonsense you are talking, Pat. I believe you suspect every one you meet. I suppose you will jump to the conclusion that this man whom Spennie is bringing down with him to-day is a criminal of some sort."

"How's that? Spennie bringing a friend?"

There was not a great deal of enthusiasm in McEachern's voice. His stepson was not a young man whom he respected very highly. Spennie regarded his stepfather with nervous apprehension, as one who would deal with his shortcomings with a vigor and severity of which his mother was incapable. The change of treatment which had begun after her marriage with the American had had an excellent effect upon him, but it had not been pleasant. As Nebuchadnezzar is reported to have said of his vegetarian diet, it may have been wholesome, but it was not good. McEachern, for his part, regarded Spennie as a boy who would get into mischief unless he had an eye fixed upon him. So he proceeded to fix that eye.

"Yes, I must be seeing Harding about getting the rooms ready. Spennie's friend is bringing his man with him."

"Who is his friend?"

"He doesn't say. He just says he's a man he met in London."

"H'm!"

"And what does that grunt mean, I should like to know? I believe you've begun to suspect the poor man already, without seeing him."

"I don't say I have. But a man can pick up strange people in London."

"Pat, you're perfectly awful. I believe you suspect every one you meet. What do you suspect me of, I wonder?"

"That's easy answered," said McEachern. "Robbery from the person."

"What have I stolen?"

"Me heart, me dear," replied McEachern gallantly, with a vast grin.

"After that," said his wife, "I think I had better go. I had no idea you could make such pretty speeches. Pat!"

"Well, me dear?"

"Don't send for that detective. It really wouldn't do. If it got about that we couldn't trust our guests, we should never live it down. You won't, will you?"

"Very well, me dear."

What followed may afford some slight clue to the secret of Mr. Patrick McEachern's rise in the world. It certainly suggests singleness of purpose, which is one of the essentials of success.

No sooner had the door closed behind Lady Jane than he went to his writing table, took pen and paper, and wrote the following letter:

To the Manager, Wragge's Detective Agency,
Holborn Bars, London, E. C.

Sir:

With ref'ce to my last of the 28th ult., I should be glad if
you would send down immediately one of your best men.
Am making arrangements to receive him. Shall be glad if
you will instruct him as follows, viz. (a) that he shall stay at
the village inn in character of American seeing sights of
England and anxious to inspect the abbey; (b) that he shall
call and ask to see me. I shall then recognize him as old
New York friend, and move his baggage from above inn to
the abbey. Yours faithfully,

P. McEACHERN.

P.S.—Kindly not send a rube, but a real smart man.

This brief but pregnant letter cost him some pains in its
composition. He was not a ready writer. But he completed it at
last to his satisfaction. There was a crisp purity in the style
which pleased him. He read it over, and put in a couple of
commas. Then he placed it in an envelope, and lit another
cigar.

CHAPTER IV

Jimmy's acquaintance with Spennie Blunt had developed rapidly in the few days following their first meeting. Spennie had called next morning to repay the loan, and two days later had invited Jimmy to come down to Shropshire with him. Which invitation, Jimmy, bored with London, had readily accepted. Spike he had decided to take with him in the role of valet. The Bowery boy was probably less fitted for the post than any one has ever been since the world began; but it would not do to leave him at Savoy Mansions.

It had been arranged that they should meet Spennie at Paddington station. Accompanied by Spike, who came within an ace of looking almost respectable in new blue serge, Jimmy arrived at Paddington with a quarter of an hour to spare. Nearly all London seemed to be at the station, with the exception of Spennie. Of that light-haired and hearted youth there were no signs. But just as the train was about to start, the missing one came skimming down the platform and hurled himself in. For the first ten minutes he sat panting. At the conclusion of that period, he spoke.

"Dash it!" he said. "I've suddenly remembered I never telegraphed home to let 'em know what train we were coming by. Now what'll happen is that there won't be anything at Corven to meet us and take us up to the abbey. And you can't get a cab. They don't grow such things."

"How far is it to walk?"

"Five solid miles. And uphill most of the way. And I've got a bad foot!"

"As a matter of fact," said Jimmy, "it's just possible that we shall be met, after all. While I was waiting for you at Paddington I heard a man asking if he had to change for Corven. He may be going to the abbey, too."

"What sort of a looking man?"

"Tall. Thin. Rather a wreck."

"Probably my Uncle Thomas. Frightful man. Always trying to roast a chap, don't, you know. Still, there's one consolation. If it is Uncle Thomas, they'll have sent the automobile for him. I shouldn't think he'd ever walked more than a hundred yards in his natural, not at a stretch. He generally stays with us in the summer. I wonder if he's bringing Aunt Julia with him. You didn't see her, I suppose, by any chance? Tall, and talks to beat the band. He married her for her money," concluded Spennie charitably.

"Isn't she attractive, either?"

"Aunt Julia," said Spennie with feeling, "is the absolute limit. Wait till you see her. Sort of woman who makes you feel that your hands are the color of a frightful tomato and the size of a billiard table, if you know what I mean. By gad, though, you should see her jewels. It's perfectly beastly the way that woman crams them on. She's got one rope of pearls which is supposed to have cost forty thousand pounds. Look out for it to-night at dinner. It's worth seeing."

Jimmy Pitt was distressed to feel distinct symptoms of a revival of the Old Adam as he listened to these alluring details. It was trying a reformed man a little high, he could not help thinking with some indignation, to dangle forty thousand pounds' worth of pearls before his eyes over the freshly turned sods of the grave of his past. It was the sort of test which might have shaken the resolution of the oldest established brand from the burning.

He could not keep his mind from dwelling on the subject. Even the fact that—commercially—there was no need for him to think of such things could not restrain him. He was rich now, and could afford to be honest. He tried to keep that fact steadily before him, but instinct was too powerful. His operations in the old days had never been conducted purely with an eye to financial profit. He had collected gems almost as much for what they were as for what they could bring. Many a time had the faithful Spike bewailed the flaw in an otherwise admirable character, which had induced his leader to keep a portion of the spoil instead of converting it at once into good dollar bills. It had had to go sooner or later, but Jimmy had always clung to it as long as possible. To Spike a diamond brooch of cunning workmanship was merely the equivalent of so many "plunks". That a man, otherwise more than sane, should value a jewel for its own sake was to him an inexplicable thing.

Jimmy was still deep in thought when the train, which had been taking itself less seriously for the last half hour, stopping at stations of quite minor importance and generally showing a tendency to dawdle, halted again. A board with the legend "Corven" in large letters showed that they had reached their destination.

"Here we are," said Spennie. "Hop out. Now what's the betting that there isn't room for all of us in the bubble?"

From farther down the train a lady and gentleman emerged.

"That's the man. Is that your uncle?" said Jimmy.

"Guilty," said Spennie gloomily. "I suppose we'd better go and tackle them. Come on."

They walked up the platform to where Sir Thomas stood

smoking a meditative cigar and watching in a dispassionate way the efforts of his wife to bully the solitary porter attached to the station into a frenzy. Sir Thomas was a very tall, very thin man, with cold eyes, and tight, thin lips. His clothes fitted him in the way clothes do fit one man in a thousand. They were the best part of him. His general appearance gave one the idea that his meals did him little good, and his meditations rather less. His conversation—of which there was not a great deal—was designed for the most part to sting. Many years' patient and painstaking sowing of his wild oats had left him at fifty-six with few pleasures; but among those that remained he ranked high the discomfiting of his neighbors.

"This is my friend Pitt, uncle," said Spennie, presenting Jimmy with a motion of the hand.

Sir Thomas extended three fingers. Jimmy extended two, and the handshake was not a success.

At this point in the interview, Spike came up, chuckling amiably, with a magazine in his hand.

"P'Chee!" said Spike. "Say, Mr. Chames, de mug what wrote dis piece must ha' bin livin' out in de woods for fair. His stunt ain't writin', sure. Say, dere's a gazebo what wants to get busy wit' de heroine's jools what's locked in de drawer in de dressin' room. So dis mug, what do youse t'ink he does? Why—"

"Another friend of yours, Spennie?" inquired Sir Thomas politely, eying the red-haired speaker with interest.

"It's—"

He looked appealingly at Jimmy.

"It's only my man," said Jimmy. "Spike," he added in an undertone, "to the woods. Chase yourself. It's not up to you to do stunts on this beat. Fade away."

P. G. Wodehouse

"Sure," said the abashed Spike, restored to a sense of his position. "Dat's right. I've got wheels in me coco, that's what I've got, comin' buttin' in here. Sorry, Mr. Chames. Sorry, gents. Me for the tall grass."

He trotted away.

"Your man seems to have a pretty taste in literature," said Sir Thomas to Jimmy. "Well, my dear, finished your chat with the porter?"

Lady Blunt had come up, flushed and triumphant, having left the solitary porter a demoralized wreck.

"I'm through," she announced crisply. "Well, Spencer? How are you? Who's this? Don't stand gaping, child. Who's your friend?"

Spennie explained with some incoherence that his name was Pitt. His uncle had shaken him; the arrival of his aunt seemed to unnerve him completely.

"Pleased to meet you," snapped Lady Blunt. "Spencer, where are your trunks? Left them behind, I suppose? No? Well, that's a surprise. Tell that porter to look after them. If you have any trouble with him, mention it to me. *I'll* make him jump around. Where's the automobile? Outside? Where? Take me to it."

Lady Blunt, when conversing, resembled a Maxim gun more than anything else in the world.

"I'm afraid," said Spennie in an abject manner, as they left the station, "that it will be rather a bit of a frightful squash—what I mean to say is, I hardly think we shall all find room in the auto. I see they have only sent the small one."

Lady Blunt stopped short, and fixed him with a glittering eye.

"I know what it is, Spencer," she said. "You never telegraphed to your mother to tell her what time you were going to arrive."

Spennie opened his mouth feebly, but apparently changing his mind, made no reply.

"My dear," said Sir Thomas smoothly, "we must not expect too much of Spennie."

"Pshaw!" This was a single shot from the Maxim.

The baited youth looked vainly for assistance to Jimmy.

"But—er—aunt," said Spennie. "Really, I—er—I only just caught the train. Didn't I, Pitt?"

"What? Oh, yes. Got in just as it was moving."

"That was it. I really hadn't time to telegraph. Had I, Pitt?"

"Not a minute."

"And how was it you were so late?"

Spennie plunged into an explanation, feeling all the time that he was making things worse for himself. Nobody is at his best in the matter of explanations if a lady whom he knows to be possessed of a firm belief in the incurable weakness of his intellect is looking fixedly at him during the recital. A prolonged conversation with Lady Blunt always made him feel exactly as if he were being tied into knots.

"All this," said Sir Thomas, as his nephew paused for breath, "is very, very characteristic of our dear Spennie."

Our dear Spennie broke into a perspiration.

"However," continued Sir Thomas, "there's room for either you or—"

"Pitt," said Jimmy. "P—i double t."

Sir Thomas bowed.

"In front with the chauffeur, if you care to take the seat."

"I'll walk," said Jimmy. "I'd rather."

"Frightfully good of you, old chap," whispered Spennie. "Sure you don't mind? I do hate walking, and my foot's hurting fearfully."

"Which is my way?"

"Straight as you can go. You go to the—"

"Spennie," said Sir Thomas suavely, "your aunt expresses a wish to arrive at the abbey in time for dinner. If you could manage to come to some arrangement about that seat—"

Spennie climbed hurriedly into the automobile. The last Jimmy saw of him was a hasty vision of him being prodded in the ribs by Lady Blunt's parasol, while its owner said something to him which, judging by his attitude, was not pleasant.

He watched them out of sight, and started to follow at a leisurely pace. It certainly was an ideal afternoon for a country walk. The sun was just hesitating whether to treat the time as afternoon or evening. Eventually it decided that it was evening, and moderated its beams. After London, the country was deliciously fresh and cool. Jimmy felt, as the scent of the hedges came to him, that the only thing worth doing in the world was to settle down somewhere with three acres and a cow, and become pastoral.

There was a marked lack of traffic on the road. Once he met a cart, and once a flock of sheep with a friendly dog. Sometimes a rabbit would dash out into the road, stop to listen, and dart into the opposite hedge, all hind legs and white scut. But except for these he was alone in the world.

And gradually there began to be borne in upon him the conviction that he had lost his way.

It is difficult to judge distance when one is walking, but it certainly seemed to Jimmy that he must have covered five miles by this time. He must have mistaken the way. He had certainly come straight. He could not have come straighter. On the other hand, it would be quite in keeping with the cheap substitute which served Spennie Blunt in place of a mind that he should have forgotten to mention some important turning. Jimmy sat down by the roadside.

As he sat, there came to him from down the road the sound of a horse's feet, trotting. He got up. Here was somebody at last who would direct him.

The sound came nearer. The horse turned the corner; and Jimmy saw with surprise that it bore no rider.

"Hullo!" he said. "Accident? And, by Jove, a side saddle!"

The curious part of it was that the horse appeared in no way a wild horse. It did not seem to be running away. It gave the impression of being out for a little trot on its own account, a sort of equine constitutional.

Jimmy stopped the horse, and led it back the way it had come. As he turned the bend in the road, he saw a girl in a riding habit running toward him. She stopped running when she caught sight of him, and slowed down to a walk.

"Thank you *so much*," she said, taking the reins from him. "Oh, Dandy, you naughty old thing."

Jimmy looked at her flushed, smiling face, and uttered an exclamation of astonishment. The girl was staring at him, open-eyed.

P. G. Wodehouse

"Molly!" he cried.

"Jimmy!"

And then a curious feeling of constraint fell simultaneously upon them both.

CHAPTER V

"How are you, Molly?"

"Quite well, thank you, Jimmy."

A pause.

"You're looking very well."

"I'm feeling very well. How are you?"

"Quite well, thanks. Very well, indeed"

Another pause.

And then their eyes met, and at the same moment they burst out laughing.

"Your manners are *beautiful*, Jimmy. And I'm so glad you're so well! What an extraordinary thing us meeting like this. I thought you were in New York."

"I thought you were. You haven't altered a bit, Molly."

"Nor have you. How queer this is! I can't understand it."

"Nor can I. I don't want to. I'm satisfied without. Do you know before I met you I was just thinking I hadn't a single friend in this country. I'm on my way to stay with a man I've only known a few days, and his people, whom I don't know at all, and a bunch of other guests, whom I've never heard of, and his uncle, who's a sort of human icicle, and his aunt, who makes you feel like thirty cents directly she starts to talk to you, and the family watchdog, who will probably bite me. But now! You must live near here or you wouldn't be chasing horses about this road."

"I live at a place called Corven Abbey."

"What Corven Abbey? Why, that's where I'm going."

"Jimmy! Oh, I see. You're Spennie's friend. But where is Spennie?"

"At the abbey by now. He went in the auto with his uncle and aunt."

"How did you meet Spennie?"

"Oh, I did a very trifling Good Samaritan act, for which he was unduly grateful, and he adopted me from that moment."

"How long have you been living in England, then? I never dreamed of you being here."

"I've been on this side about a week. If you want my history in a nutshell, it's this. Rich uncle. Poor nephew. Deceased uncle. Rich nephew. I'm a man with money now. Lots of money."

"How nice for you, Jimmy. Father came into money, too. That's how I come to be over here. I wish you and father had got on better together."

"Your father, my dear Molly, has a manner with people he is not fond of which purists might call slightly abrupt. Perhaps things will be different, now."

The horse gave a sudden whinny.

"I wish you wouldn't do that sort of thing without warning," said Jimmy to it plaintively.

"He knows he's near home, and he knows it's his dinner time. There, now you can see the abbey. How do you like it?"

They had reached a point in the road where the fields to the right sloped sharply downward. A few hundred yards away, backed by woods, stood the beautiful home which ex-Policeman McEachern had caused to be builded for him. The setting sun lit up the waters of the lake. No figures were to be seen moving in the grounds. The place resembled a palace of sleep.

"Well?" said Molly.

"By Jove!"

"Isn't it?" said Molly. "I'm so glad you like it. I always feel as if I had invented everything round here. It hurts me if people don't appreciate it. Once I took Sir Thomas Blunt up here. It was as much as I could do to induce him to come at all. He simply won't walk. When we got to where we are standing now, I pointed and said: 'There!'"

"And what did he do? Moan with joy?"

"He grunted, and said it struck him as rather rustic."

"Beast! I met Sir Thomas when we got off the train. Spennie Blunt introduced me to him. He seemed to bear it pluckily, but with some difficulty. I think we had better be going, or they will be sending out search parties."

"By the way, Jimmy," said Molly, as they went down the hill. "Can you act?"

"Can I what?"

"Act. In theatricals, you know."

"I've never tried. But I've played poker, which I should think is much the same."

"We are going to do a play, and we want another man. The man who was going to play one of the parts has had to go back to London."

"Poor devil! Fancy having to leave a place like this and go back to that dingy, overrated town."

* * * * *

The big drawing-room of the abbey was full when they arrived. Tea was going on in a desultory manner. In a chair at the far end of the room, Sir Thomas Blunt surveyed the scene gloomily through the smoke of a cigarette. The sound of Lady Blunt's voice had struck their ears as they opened the door. The Maxim gun was in action with no apparent prospect of jamming. The target of the moment was a fair, tired-looking lady, with a remarkable resemblance to Spennie. Jimmy took her to be his hostess. There was a resigned expression on her face, which he thoroughly understood. He sympathized with her.

The other occupants of the room stared for a moment at Jimmy in the austere manner peculiar to the Briton who sees a stranger, and then resumed their respective conversations. One of their number, a slight, pale, young man, as scientifically clothed as Sir Thomas, left his group, and addressed himself to Molly.

"Ah, here you are, Miss McEachern," he said. "At last. We were all getting so anxious."

"Really?" said Molly. "That's very kind of you, Mr. Wesson."

"I assure you, yes. Positively. A gray gloom had settled upon us. We pictured you in all sorts of horrid situations. I was just going to call for volunteers to scour the country, or whatever it is that one does in such circumstances. I used to read about it in books, but I have forgotten the technical term. I am relieved to find that you are not even dusty, though it would have been more romantic if you could have managed a little dust here and there. But don't consider my feelings, Miss McEachern, please."

Molly introduced Jimmy to the newcomer. They shook hands, Jimmy with something of the wariness of a boxer in the ring. He felt an instinctive distrust of this man. Why, he could not have said. Perhaps it was a certain subtle familiarity in his manner of speaking to Molly that annoyed him. Jimmy objected strongly to any one addressing her as if there existed between them some secret understanding. Already the mood of the old New York days was strong upon him. His instinct then had been to hate all her male acquaintances with an unreasoning hatred. He found himself in much the same frame of mind, now.

"So you're Spennie's friend," said Mr. Wesson, "the man who's going to show us all how to act, what?"

"I believe there is some idea of my being a 'confused noise without', or something."

"Haven't they asked you to play *Lord Algernon*?" inquired Wesson, with more animation than he usually allowed himself to exhibit.

"Who is *Lord Algernon*?"

"Only a character in the piece we are acting."

"What does he do?"

"He talks to me most of the time," said Molly.

"Then," said Jimmy decidedly, "I seem to see myself making a big hit."

"It's a long part if you aren't used to that sort of thing," said Wesson.

He had hoped that the part with its wealth of opportunity would have fallen to himself.

"I am used to it," said Jimmy. "Thanks."

"If that little beast's after Molly," thought Jimmy, "there will be trouble."

"Come along," said Molly, "and be introduced, and get some tea."

"Well, Molly, dear," said Lady Jane, with a grateful smile at the interruption, "we didn't know what had become of you. Did Dandy give you trouble?"

"Dandy's a darling, and wouldn't do anything of the sort if you asked him to. He's a kind little 'oss, as Thomas says. He only walked away when I got off to pick some roses, and I couldn't catch him. And then I met Jimmy."

Jimmy bowed.

"I hope you aren't tired out," said Lady Jane to him. "We thought you would never arrive. It's such a long walk. It was really too careless of Spennie not to let us know when he expected you."

"I was telling Spencer in the automobile," put in Lady Blunt, with ferocity, "that *my* father would have horsewhipped him if he had been a son of his. He would."

"Really, Julia!" protested Lady Jane rather faintly.

"That's so. And I don't care who knows it. A boy doesn't want to forget things if he's going to make his way in the world. I told Spencer so in the automobile."

Jimmy had noticed that Spennie was not in the room. He now understood his absence. After the ride he had probably felt that an hour or two passed out of his aunt's society would not do him any harm. He was now undergoing a rest cure, Jimmy imagined, in the billiard room.

"I can assure you," said he, by way of lending a helping hand to the absent one, "I really preferred to walk. I have only just landed in England from New York, and it's quite a treat to walk on an English country road again."

"Are you from New York? I wonder if—"

"Jimmy's an old friend," said Molly. "We knew him very well indeed. It was such a surprise meeting him."

"How interesting," said Lady Jane languidly, as if the intellectual strain of the conversation had been too much for her. "You will have such lots to talk about, won't you?"

"I say," said Jimmy, as they moved away, "who is that fellow Wesson?"

"Oh, a man," said Molly vaguely.

"There's no need to be fulsome," said Jimmy. "He can't hear."

"Mother likes him. I don't."

"Mother?"

"Hullo," said Molly, "there's father."

The door had opened while they were talking, and Mr. Patrick McEachern had walked solidly into the room. The ornaments

P. G. Wodehouse

on the Chippendale tables jingled as he came. Secretly he was somewhat embarrassed at finding himself in the midst of so many people. He had not yet mastered the art of feeling at home in his own house. At meals he did not fear his wife's guests so much. Their attention was in a manner distributed at such times, instead of being, as now, focused upon himself. He stood there square and massive, outwardly the picture of all that was rugged and independent, looking about him for a friendly face. To offer a general remark, or to go boldly and sit down beside one of those dazzling young ladies, like some heavyweight spider beside a Miss Muffet, was beyond him. In his time he had stopped runaway horses, clubbed mad dogs, and helped to break up East Side gang fights, when the combatants on both sides were using their guns lavishly and impartially; but his courage failed him here.

"Why," said Jimmy, "is your father here, too? I didn't know that."

To himself he reviled his luck. How much would he see of Molly now? Her father's views on himself were no sealed book to him.

Molly looked at him in surprise.

"Didn't know?" she said. "Didn't I tell you the place belonged to father?"

"What!" said Jimmy. "This house?"

"Yes. Of course."

"And—by gad, I've got it. He has married Spennie Blunt's mother."

"Yes."

"Well, I'm—surprised."

Suddenly he began to chuckle.

"What *is* it, Jimmy?"

"Why—why, I've just grasped the fact that your father—your father, mind you—is my host. I'm the honored guest. At his house!"

The chuckle swelled into a laugh. The noise attracted McEachern's attention, and, looking in the direction whence it proceeded, he caught sight of Molly.

With a grin of joy, he made for the sofa.

"Well, father, dear?" said Molly nervously.

Mr. McEachern was staring horribly at Jimmy, who had risen to his feet.

"How do you do, Mr. McEachern?"

The ex-policeman continued to stare.

"Father," said Molly in distress. "Father, let me present—I mean, don't you remember Jimmy? You must remember Jimmy, father! Jimmy Pitt, whom you used to know in New York."

CHAPTER VI

On his native asphalt there are few situations capable of throwing the New York policeman off his balance. In that favored clime, *savoir faire* is represented by a shrewd left hook at the jaw, and a masterful stroke of the truncheon amounts to a satisfactory repartee. Thus shall you never take the policeman of Manhattan without his answer. In other surroundings, Mr. Patrick McEachern would have known how to deal with his young acquaintance, Mr. Jimmy Pitt. But another plan of action was needed here. First of all, the hints on etiquette with which Lady Jane had favored him, from time to time, and foremost came the mandate: "Never make a scene." Scenes, Lady Jane had explained—on the occasion of his knocking down an objectionable cabman during their honeymoon trip—were of all things what polite society most resolutely abhorred. The natural man in him must be bound in chains. The sturdy blow must give way to the honeyed word. A cold "Really!" was the most vigorous retort that the best circles would countenance.

It had cost Mr. McEachern some pains to learn this lesson, but he had done it; and he proceeded on the present occasion to conduct himself high and disposedly, according to instructions from headquarters.

The surprise of finding an old acquaintance in this company rendered him dumb for a brief space, during which Jimmy looked after the conversation.

"How do you do, Mr. McEachern?" inquired Jimmy genially. "Quite a surprise meeting you in England. A pleasant surprise. By the way, one generally shakes hands in the smartest circles. Yours seem to be down there somewhere. Might I trouble you? Right. Got it? Thanks!"

He bent forward, possessed himself of Mr. McEachern's right hand, which was hanging limply at its proprietor's side, shook it warmly, and replaced it.

"'Wahye?" asked Mr. McEachern gruffly, giving a pleasing air of novelty to the hackneyed salutation by pronouncing it as one word. He took some little time getting into his stride when carrying on polite conversation.

"Very well, thank you. You're looking as strong as ever, Mr. McEachern."

The ex-policeman grunted. In a conversational sense, he was sparring for wind.

Molly had regained her composure by this time. Her father was taking the thing better than she had expected.

"It's Jimmy, father, dear," she said. "Jimmy Pitt."

"Dear old James," murmured the visitor.

"I know, me dear, I know. Wahye?"

"Still well," replied Jimmy cheerfully. "Sitting up, you will notice," he added, waving a hand in the direction of his teacup, "and taking nourishment. No further bulletins will be issued."

"Jimmy is staying here, father. He is the friend Spennie was bringing."

"This is the friend that Spennie brought," said Jimmy in a

rapid undertone. "This is the maiden all forlorn who crossed the seas, and lived in the house that sheltered the friend that Spennie brought."

"I see, me dear," said Mr. McEachern slowly. "'Wah—"

"No, I've guessed that one already," said Jimmy. "Ask me another."

Molly looked reproachfully at him. His deplorable habit of chaffing her father had caused her trouble in the old days. It may be admitted that this recreation of Jimmy's was not in the best taste; but it must also be remembered that the relations between the two had always been out of the ordinary. Great as was his affection for Molly, Jimmy could not recollect a time when war had not been raging in a greater or lesser degree between the ex-policeman and himself.

"It is very kind of you to invite me down here," said he. "We shall be able to have some cozy chats over old times when I was a wanderer on the face of the earth, and you—"

"Yis, yis," interrupted Mr. McEachern hastily, "somewhere ilse, aftherward."

"You shall choose time and place, of course. I was only going to ask you how you liked leaving the—"

"United States?" put in Mr. McEachern, with an eagerness which broadened his questioner's friendly smile, as the Honorable Louis Wesson came toward them.

"Well, I'm not after saying it was not a wrinch at firrst, but I considered it best to lave Wall Street—Wall Street, ye understand, before—"

"I see. Before you fell a victim to the feverish desire for reckless speculation which is so marked a characteristic of the American business man, what?"

"That's it," said the other, relieved.

"I, too, have been speculating," said Mr. Wesson, "as to whether you would care to show me the rose garden, Miss McEachern, as you promised yesterday. Of all flowers, I love roses best. You remember Bryant's lines, Miss McEachern? 'The rose that lives its little hour is prized beyond the sculptured flower.'"

Jimmy interposed firmly. "I'm very sorry," he said, "but the fact is Miss McEachern has just promised to take me with her to feed the fowls.

"I gamble on fowls," he thought. "There must be some in a high-class establishment of this kind."

"I'd quite forgotten," said Molly.

"I thought you had. We'd better start at once. Nothing upsets a fowl more than having to wait for dinner."

"Nonsense, me dear Molly," said Mr. McEachern bluffly. "Run along and show Mr. Wesson the roses. Nobody wants to waste time over a bunch of hens."

"Perhaps not," said Jimmy thoughtfully, "perhaps not. I might be better employed here, amusing the people by telling them all about our old New York days and—"

Mr. McEachern might have been observed, and was so observed by Jimmy, to swallow somewhat convulsively.

"But as Molly promised ye—" said he.

"Just so," said Jimmy. "My own sentiments, neatly expressed. Shall we start, Miss McEachern?"

"That fellah," said Mr. Wesson solemnly to his immortal soul, "is a damn bounder. *And* cad," he added after a moment's reflection.

The fowls lived in a little world of noise and smells at the back of the stables. The first half of the journey thither was performed in silence. Molly's cheerful little face was set in what she probably imagined to be a forbidding scowl. The tilt of her chin spoke of displeasure.

"If a penny would be any use to you," said Jimmy, breaking the tension.

"I'm not at all pleased with you," said Molly severely.

"How *can* you say such savage things! And me an orphan, too! What's the trouble? What have I done?"

"You know perfectly well. Making fun of father like that."

"My dear girl, he loved it. Brainy badinage of that sort is exchanged every day in the best society. You should hear dukes and earls! The wit! the *esprit*! The flow of soul! Mine is nothing to it. What's this in the iron pot? Is this what you feed them? Queer birds, hens—I wouldn't touch the stuff for a fortune. It looks perfectly poisonous. Flock around, you pullets. Come in your thousands. All bad nuts returned, and a souvenir goes with every corpse. A little more of this putrescent mixture for you, sir. Certainly, pick up your dead, pick up your dead."

An unwilling dimple appeared on Molly's chin, like a sunbeam through clouds.

"All the same," she said, "you ought to be ashamed of yourself, Jimmy."

"I haven't time when I find myself stopping in the same house with a girl I've been looking for for three years."

Molly looked away. There was silence for a moment.

"Used you ever to think of me?" she said quietly.

That curious constraint which had fallen upon Jimmy in the road came to him again, now, as sobering as a blow. Something which he could not define had changed the atmosphere. Suddenly in an instant, like a shallow stream that runs babbling over the stones into some broad, still pool, the note of their talk had deepened.

"Yes," he said simply. He could find no words for what he wished to say.

"I've thought of you—often," said Molly.

He took a step toward her. But the moment had passed. Her mood had changed in a flash, or seemed to have changed. The stream babbled on over the stones again.

"Be careful, Jimmy! You nearly touched me with the spoon. I don't want to be covered with that horrible stuff. Look at that poor, little chicken out there in the cold. It hasn't had a morsel."

Jimmy responded to her lead. There was nothing else for him to do.

"It's in luck," he said.

"Give it a spoonful."

"It can have one if it likes. But it's taking big risks. Here you are, Hercules. Pitch in."

He scraped the last spoonful out of the iron pot, and they began to walk back to the house.

"You're very quiet, Jimmy," said Molly.

"I was thinking."

P. G. Wodehouse

"What about?"

"Lots of things."

"New York?"

"That among others."

"Dear old New York," said Molly, with a little sigh. "I'm not sure it wasn't—I mean, I sometimes wish—oh, you know. I mean it's lovely here, but it *was* nice in the old days, wasn't it, Jimmy? It's a pity that things change, isn't it?"

"It depends."

"What do you mean?"

"I don't mind things changing, if people don't."

"Do you think I've changed? You said I hadn't when we met in the road."

"You haven't, as far as looks go."

"Have I changed in other ways?"

Jimmy looked at her.

"I don't know," he said slowly.

They were in the hall, now. Keggs had just left after beating the dressing gong. The echoes of it still lingered. Molly paused on the bottom step.

"I haven't, Jimmy," she said; and ran on up the stairs.

CHAPTER VII

Jimmy dressed for dinner in a very exalted frame of mind that night. It seemed to him that he had awakened from a sort of a stupor. Life was so much fuller of possibilities than he had imagined a few days back. The sudden acquisition of his uncle's money had, in a manner, brought him to a halt. Till then the exhilarating feeling of having his hand against the world had lent a zest to life. There had been no monotony. There had always been obstacles. One may hardly perhaps dilate on the joys of toil in connection with him, considering the precise methods by which he had supported himself; but nevertheless his emotions when breaking the law of the United States had been akin to those of the honest worker in so far that his operations had satisfied the desire for action which possesses every man of brains and energy. They had given him something to do. He had felt alive. His uncle's legacy had left him with a sensation of abrupt stoppage. Life had suddenly become aimless.

But now everything was altered. Once more the future was a thing of importance, to-morrow a day to be looked forward to with keen expectation.

He tried to throw his mind back to the last occasion when he had seen Molly. He could not remember that he had felt any excessive emotion. Between *camaraderie* and love there is a broad gulf. It had certainly never been bridged in the old New York days. Then the frank friendliness of which the American girl appears to have the monopoly had been Molly's chief charm in his eyes. It had made possible a comradeship such as might have existed between men. But now there was a difference. England seemed to have brought about a subtle change in her. Instinctively he felt that the old friendship, adequate before, was not enough now. He wanted more. The unexpected meeting, following so closely upon Spike's careless words in London, had shown him his true feelings. Misgivings crept upon him. Had he a right? Was it fair? He looked back at the last eight years of his life with the eye of an impartial judge. He saw them stripped of the glamour which triumphant cunning had lent them; saw them as they would appear to Molly.

He scowled at his reflection in the glass. "You've been a bad lot, my son," he said. "There's only one thing in your favor; and that is the fact that you've cut it all out for keeps. We must be content with that."

There was a furtive rap at the door. "Hullo?" said Jimmy. "Yes?"

The door opened slowly. A grin, surmounted by a mop of red hair, appeared round the edge of it.

"Well, Spike. Come in. What's the matter?"

The rest of Mr. Mullins entered the room.

"Gee, Mr. Chames, I wasn't sure dat dis was your room. Say, who do youse t'ink I nearly bumped me coco ag'in out in de corridor? Why, old man McEachern, de cop. Dat's right!"

"Yes?"

"Sure. Say, what's he doin' on dis beat? Youse c'u'd have knocked me down wit' a bit of poiper when I see him. I pretty near went down and out. Dat's right. Me heart ain't got back home yet."

"Did he recognize you?"

"Sure! He starts like an actor on top de stoige when he sees he's up against de plot to ruin him, an' he gives me de fierce eye."

"Well?"

"I was wondering was I on Third Avenue, or was I standing on me coco, or what was I doin', anyhow. Den I slips off and chases meself up here. Say, Mr. Chames, can *youse* put me wise? What's de game? What's old man McEachern doin' stunts dis side for?"

"It's all right, Spike. Keep calm. I can explain. Mr. McEachern owns the house."

"On your way, Mr. Chames! What's dat?"

"This is his house we're in, now. He left the force three years ago, came over here, and bought this place. And here we are again, all gathered together under the same roof, like a jolly little family party."

Spike's open mouth bore witness to his amazement.

"Den all dis—"

"Belongs to him? That's it. We are his guests, Spike."

"But what's he goin' to do?"

"I couldn't say. I'm expecting to hear shortly. But we needn't worryourselves. The next move's with him. If he wants to say anything about it, he must come to me."

"Sure. It's up to him," agreed Spike.

"I'm quite comfortable. Speaking for myself, I'm having a good time. How are you getting on downstairs?"

"De limit, Mr. Chames. Honest, I'm on pink velvet. Dey's an

old gazebo, de butler, Keggs his name is, dat's de best ever at handing out long woids. I sit and listen. Dey calls me Mr. Mullins down dere," said Spike, with pride.

"Good. I'm glad you're all right. There's no reason why we shouldn't have an excellent time here. I don't think that Mr. McEachern will turn us out, after he's heard one or two little things I have to say to him. Just a few reminiscences of the past which may interest him. I have the greatest affection for Mr. McEachern, though he did club me once with his night stick; but nothing shall make me stir from here for the next week at any rate."

"Not on your life," agreed Spike. "Say, Mr. Chames, he must have got a lot of plunks to buy dis place. And I know how he got dem, too. Dat's right. I comes from old New York meself."

"Hush, Spike, this is scandal!"

"Sure," said the Bowery boy doggedly, securely mounted now on his favorite hobby horse. "I knows, and youse knows, Mr. Chames. Gee, I wish I'd bin a cop. But I wasn't tall enough. Dey's de fellers wit' de long green in der banks. Look at dis old McEachern. Money to boin a wet dog wit', he's got, and never a bit of woik for it from de start to de finish. An' look at me, Mr. Chames."

"I do, Spike, I do."

"Look at me. Getting busy all de year round, woiking to beat de band all—"

"In prisons oft," said Jimmy.

"Dat's right. And chased all roun' de town. And den what? Why, to de bad at de end of it all. Say, it's enough to make a feller—"

"Turn honest." said Jimmy. "You've hit it, Spike. You'll be

glad some day that you reformed."

But on this point Spike seemed to be doubtful. He was silent for a moment; then, as if following upon a train of thoughts, he said: "Mr. Chames, dis is a fine big house."

"Splendid!"

"Say, couldn't we—"

"Spike!" said Jimmy warningly.

"Well, couldn't we?" said Spike doggedly. "It ain't often youse butts into a dead-easy proposition like dis one. We shouldn't have to do a t'ing excep' git busy. De stuff's just lying about, Mr. Chames."

"I have noticed it."

"Aw, it's a waste to leave it."

"Spike," said Jimmy, "I warned you of this. I begged you to be on your guard, to fight against your professional instincts; and you must do it. I know it's hard, but it's got to be done. Try and occupy your mind. Collect butterflies."

Spike shuffled in gloomy silence.

"'Member dose jools we got in de hotel de year before I was copped?" he asked at length irrelevantly.

Jimmy finished tying his tie, looked at the result for a moment in the glass, then replied: "Yes, I remember."

"We got anudder key dat fitted de door. 'Member dat?"

Jimmy nodded.

"And some of dose knock-out drops. What's dat? Chloryform?

Dat's right. An' we didn't do a t'ing else. An' we lived for de rest of de year on dose jools."

Spike paused.

"Dat was to de good," he said wistfully.

Jimmy made no reply.

"Dere's a loidy here," continued Spike, addressing the chest of drawers, "dat's got a necklace of jools what's wort' two hundred thousand plunks."

"I know."

Silence again.

"Two hundred thousand plunks," breathed Spike.

"What a necklace!" thought Jimmy.

"Keggs told me dat. De old gazebo what hands out de long woids. I could find out where dey're kept dead easy.'

"What a king of necklaces!" thought Jimmy.

"Shall I, Mr. Chames?"

"Shall you what?" asked Jimmy, coming out of his thoughts with a start.

"Why, find out where de loidy keeps de jools."

"Confound you, Spike! How often am I to tell you that I have done with all that sort of thing forever? I never want to see or touch another stone that doesn't belong to me. I don't want to hear about them. They don't interest me."

"Sorry, Mr. Chames. But dey must cop de limit for fair, dose jools. Two hundred t'ousand plunks! What's dat dis side?"

"Forty thousand pounds," said Jimmy shortly. "Now, drop it."

"Yes, Mr. Chames. Can I help youse wit' de duds?"

"No, thanks. Spike; I'm through, now. You might just give me a brush down, though, if you don't mind. Not that. That's a hair brush. Try the big black one."

"Dis is a dude suit for fair," observed Spike, pausing in his labors.

"Glad you like it, Spike."

"It's de limit. Excuse me. How much of de long green did youse pungle for it, Mr. Chames?"

"I really can't remember," said Jimmy, with a laugh. "I could look up the bill and let you know. Seventy guineas, I fancy."

"What's dat—guineas? Is dat more dan a pound?"

"A shilling more. Why?"

Spike resumed his brushing.

"What a lot of dude suits youse could get," he observed meditatively, "if youse had dose jools."

"Oh, *curse* the jewels for the hundredth time!" snapped Jimmy.

"Yes, Mr. Chames. But, say, dat must be a boid of a necklace, dat one. You'll be seeing it at de dinner, Mr. Chames."

Whatever comment Jimmy might have made on this insidious statement was checked by a sudden bang on the door. Almost simultaneously the handle turned.

"P'Chee!" cried Spike. "It's de cop!"

Jimmy smiled pleasantly.

"Come in, Mr. McEachern," he said, "come in. Journeys end in lovers meeting. You know my friend, Mr. Mullins, I think? Shut the door, and sit down and let's talk of many things."

CHAPTER VIII

"It's a conspiracy!" thundered Mr. McEachern.

He stood in the doorway, breathing heavily. It has been shown that the ex-policeman was somewhat prone to harbor suspicions of those round about him, and at the present moment his mind was aflame. Indeed, a more trusting man might have been excused for feeling a little doubtful as to the intentions of Jimmy and Spike. When McEachern had heard that his stepson had brought home a casual London acquaintance, he had suspected the existence of hidden motives on the part of the unknown. Spennie, he had told himself, was precisely the sort of youth to whom the professional bunko-steerer would attach himself with shouts of joy. Never, he had assured himself, had there been a softer proposition than his stepson since bunko-steering became a profession.

When he found that the strange visitor was Jimmy Pitt, his suspicions had increased a thousandfold.

And when, going to his dressing room to get ready for dinner, he had nearly run into Spike Mullins, Red Spike of shameful memory, his frame of mind had been that of a man to whom a sudden ray of light reveals the fact that he is on the very brink of a black precipice. Jimmy and Spike had been a firm in New York. And here they were, together again, in his house in Shropshire. To say that the thing struck McEachern as sinister is to put the matter baldly. There was once a gentleman who remarked that he smelt a rat and saw it floating in the air.

P. G. Wodehouse

Ex-constable McEachern smelt a regiment of rats, and the air seemed to him positively congested with them.

His first impulse had been to rush to Jimmy's room there and then; but Lady Jane had trained him well. Though the heavens might fall, he must not be late for dinner. So he went and dressed, and an obstinate tie put the finishing touches to his wrath.

Jimmy regarded him coolly, without moving from the chair in which he had seated himself. Spike, on the other hand, seemed embarrassed. He stood first on one leg and then on the other, as if he were testing the respective merits of each, and would make a definite choice later on.

"Ye scoundrels!" growled McEachern.

Spike, who had been standing for a few moments on his right leg, and seemed at last to have come to a decision, hastily changed to the left, and grinned feebly.

"Say, youse won't want me any more, Mr. Chames?" he whispered.

"No; you can go, Spike."

"Ye stay where y'are, ye red-headed limb."

"Run along, Spike!" said Jimmy.

The Bowery boy looked doubtfully at the huge form of the ex-policeman, which blocked access to the door.

"Would you mind letting my man pass?" said Jimmy.

"Ye stay—" began McEachern.

Jimmy got up, and walked round him to the door, which he opened. Spike shot out like a rabbit released from a trap. He was not lacking in courage, but he disliked embarrassing interviews, and it struck him that Mr. Chames was the man to handle a situation of this kind. He felt that he himself would only be in the way.

"Now we can talk comfortably," said Jimmy, going back to his chair.

McEachern's deep-set eyes gleamed, and his forehead grew red; but he mastered his feelings.

"An' now," said he, "perhaps ye'll explain!"

"What exactly?" asked Jimmy.

"What ye're doin' here."

"Nothing at the moment."

"Ye know what I mane. Why are ye here, you and that red-headed devil?"

He jerked his head in the direction of the door.

"I am here because I was very kindly invited to come by your stepson."

"I know ye."

"You have that privilege."

"I know ye, I say, and I want to know what ye're here to do."

"To do? Well, I shall potter about the garden, don't you know, and smell the roses, and look at the horses, and feed the chickens, and perhaps go for an occasional row on the lake. Nothing more. Oh, yes, I believe they want me to act in these theatricals."

"An' I'll tell ye another thing ye'll be wanted to do, and that is to go away from here at wance!"

"My dear old sir!"

"Ye hear me? At wance."

"Couldn't think of it," said Jimmy decidedly. "Not for a moment."

"I'll expose ye," stormed McEachern. "I'll expose ye. Will ye deny that ye was a crook in New York?"

"What proofs have you?"

"Proofs! Will you deny it?"

"No. It's quite true."

"I knew it."

"But I'm a reformed character, now, Mr. McEachern. I have money of my own. It was left me. I hear you had money left you, too."

"I did," said McEachern shortly.

"Congratulate you. I'm glad I know, because otherwise I might have formed quite a wrong impression when I came here and found you with money to burn. Quite the old English squire now, Mr. McEachern, what?"

"Ye'll lave the house to-morrow."

"All the more reason why we should make the most of this opportunity of talking over old times. Did you mind leaving the force?"

"And ye'll take that blackguard Mullins wid ye."

"Judging from the stories one hears, it must be a jolly sort of life. What a pity so many of them go in for graft. I could tell you some stories about a policeman I used to know in New York. He was the champion grafter. I remember hearing one yarn from a newspaper man out there. This reporter chap happened to hear of the grumblings of some tenants of an apartment house uptown which led them to believe that certain noises they complained of were made by burglars who used the flat as a place to pack up the loot for shipment to other cities. You know that habit of ours, don't you? He was quite right, and when he tipped off his newspaper they reported the thing to the police. Now, I could have gone right up and made those men show up their hands by merely asking them to.

"Not so the police. I wonder if you remember the case. You look as if you were beginning to. The police went blundering at wrong doors, and most of the gang got away. And while they were in the house after the raid a woman was able to slip in and take away on an express wagon the three trunks which were to have been held for evidence. And that's not all, either. There was one particular policeman who held the case for the prosecution in his hands. If he had played up in court next day, the one man that had been captured would have got all that was coming to him. What happened? Why, his evidence broke down, and the man was discharged. It's a long story. I hope it hasn't bored you."

McEachern did not look bored. He was mopping his forehead, and breathing quickly.

"It was a most interesting case," said Jimmy. "I've got all the names."

"It's a lie!"

"Not at all. True as anything. Ever heard of that policeman—I've got his name, too—who made a lot of money by getting appointments in the force for men of his acquaintance? He used to be paid heavily for it, and you'd hardly believe what a lot of scoundrels he let in in that way."

"See here—" began McEachern huskily.

"I wonder if you ever came across any men in the force who made anything by that dodge of arresting a person and then getting a lawyer for them. Ever heard of that? It's rather like a double ruff at bridge. You—I'm awfully sorry. I shouldn't have used that word. What I meant to say was the policeman makes his arrest, then suggests that the person had better have a bondsman. He gathers in a bondsman, who charges the prisoner four dollars for bailing him out. Two dollars of this goes to the sergeant, who accepts the bail without question, and the policeman takes one. Then the able and intelligent officer says to the prisoner: 'What you want is a lawyer.' 'Right,' says the prisoner, 'if you think so.' Off goes the policeman and gets the lawyer. Five more dollars, of which he gets his share. It's a beautiful system. It might interest the people at dinner to-night to hear about it. I think I'll tell them."

"You'll—"

"And when you come to think that some policemen in New York take tribute from peddlers who obstruct the traffic, tradesmen who obstruct the sidewalk, restaurant keepers who keep open after one o'clock in the morning, drivers who exceed speed limits, and keepers of pool rooms, you'll understand that there's a good bit to be made out of graft, if you go in for it seriously. It's uncommonly lucky, McEachern, that you were left that money. Otherwise you might have been tempted, mightn't you?"

There was a somewhat breathless silence in the room. Mr. McEachern was panting slightly.

"You couldn't reconsider your decision about sending me away to-morrow, I suppose?" said Jimmy, flicking at his shoes with a handkerchief. "It's a lovely part of the country, this. I would be sorry to leave it."

Mr. McEachern's brain was working with unwonted rapidity. This man must be silenced at all costs. It would be fatal to his prospects in English society if one tithe of these gruesome stories were made public. And he believed Jimmy capable of making them public, being guilty thereby of an error of judgment. Jimmy, though he had no respect at all for Mr. McEachern, would have died sooner than spread any story which, even in an indirect way, could reflect upon Molly. Mr. McEachern, however, had not the advantage of knowing his antagonist's feelings, and the bluff was successful.

"Ye can stay," he said.

"Thanks," said Jimmy.

"And I'll beg ye not to mention the force at dinner or at any other time."

"I won't dream of it."

"They think I made me money on Wall Street."

"It would have been a slower job there. You were wise in your choice. Shall we go down to the drawing-room, now?"

"Ye say y'are rich yerself," said McEachern.

"Very," said Jimmy, "so don't you worry yourself, my Wall Street speculator."

Mr. McEachern did not worry himself. He had just recollected that in a very short time he would have a trained detective on the premises. Any looking after that James Willoughby Pitt might require might safely be left in the hands of this expert.

P. G. Wodehouse

CHAPTER IX

It was at dinner that Jimmy had his first chance of seeing the rope of pearls which had so stimulated the roving fancy of Spike Mullins. Lady Blunt sat almost opposite to him. Her dress was of unrelieved black, and formed a wonderfully effective foil to the gems. It was not a rope of pearls. It was a collar. Her neck was covered with them. There was something Oriental and barbaric in the overwhelming display of jewelry. And this suggestion of the East was emphasized by the wearer's regal carriage. Lady Blunt knew when she looked well. She did not hold herself like one apologizing for venturing to exist.

Jimmy stared hungrily across the table. The room was empty to him but for that gleaming mass of gems. He breathed softly and quickly through clinched teeth.

"Jimmy!" whispered a voice.

It seemed infinitely remote.

A hand shook his elbow gently. He started.

"*Don't* stare like that, *please*. What is the matter?"

Molly, seated at his side, was looking at him wide-eyed. Jimmy smiled with an effort. Every nerve in his body seemed to be writhing.

"Sorry," he said. "I'm only hungry. I always look like that at the beginning of a meal."

"Well, here comes Keggs with some soup for you. You'd better not waste another moment. You looked perfectly awful."

"No!"

"Like a starved wolf."

"You must look after me," said Jimmy, "see that the wolf's properly fed."

* * * * *

The conversation, becoming general with the fish, was not of a kind to remove from Jimmy's mind the impression made by the sight of the pearls. It turned on crime in general and burglary in particular.

Spennie began it.

"Oh, I say," he said, "I forgot to tell you, mother. Number Six was burgled the other night."

Number Six-a, Easton Square, was the family's London house.

"Burgled!"

"Well, broken into," said Spennie, gratified to find that he had got the ear of his entire audience. Even Lady Blunt was silent and attentive. "Chap got in through the scullery window about one o'clock, in the morning. It was the night after you dined with me, Pitt."

"And what did our Spennie do?" inquired Sir Thomas.

"Oh, I—er—I was out at the time," said Spennie. "But something frightened the feller," he went on hurriedly, "and he made a bolt for it without taking anything."

P. G. Wodehouse

Jimmy, looking down the table, became conscious that his host's eye was fixed gloomily upon him. He knew intuitively what was passing in McEachern's mind. The ex-policeman was feeling that his worst suspicions had been confirmed. Jimmy had dined with Spennie—obviously a mere excuse for spying out the land; and the very next night the house had been burgled. Once more Mr. McEachern congratulated himself on his astuteness in engaging the detective from Wragge's Agency. With Jimmy above stairs and Spike Mullins below, that sleuthhound would have his hands full.

"Burglary," said Wesson, leaning back and taking advantage of a pause, "is the hobby of the sportsman and the life work of the avaricious."

Everybody seemed to have something to say on the subject. One young lady gave it as her opinion that she would not like to find a burglar under her bed. Somebody else had known a man whose father had fired at the butler, under the impression that he was a housebreaker, and had broken a valuable bust of Socrates. Spennie knew a man at Oxford whose brother wrote lyrics for musical comedy, and had done one about a burglar's best friend being his mother.

"Life," said Wesson, who had had time for reflection, "is a house which we all burgle. We enter it uninvited, take all that we can lay hands on, and go out again."

"This man's brother I was telling you about," said Spennie, "says there's only one rhyme in the English language to 'burglar', and that's 'gurgler'. Unless you count 'pergola', he says—"

"Personally," said Jimmy, with a glance at McEachern, "I have rather a sympathy for burglars. After all, they are one of the hardest-working classes in existence. They toil while everybody else is asleep. They are generally thorough sportsmen. Besides, a burglar is only a practical socialist. Philosophers talk a lot about the redistribution of wealth. The burglar goes out and does it. I have found burglars some of the decentest criminals I have ever met. Out of business hours they are charming."

"I despise burglars!" ejaculated Lady Blunt, with a suddenness which stopped Jimmy's eloquence as if a tap had been turned off. "If I found one coming after my jewels and I had a gun handy, I'd shoot him. I would."

"My dear Julia!" said Lady Jane. "Why suggest such dreadful things? At any rate, this house has never been burgled, and I don't think it's likely to be."

"Beroofen!" said Jimmy, touching the back of his chair. As he did so, he met McEachern's eye, and smiled kindly at him. The ex-policeman was looking at him with the gaze of a baffled but malignant basilisk.

"I take very good care no one gets a chance at my jewels," said Lady Blunt. "I've had a steel box made for me with a special lock which would drive the cunningest burglar on this earth mad before he'd been at it ten minutes. It would. He'd go right away and reform."

Jimmy's lips closed tightly, and a combative look came into his eye at this unconscious challenge. This woman was too aggressively confident. A small lesson. He could return the jewels by post. It would give her a much-needed jolt.

Then he pulled himself up.

"James, my boy," he said to himself, with severity, "this is hypocrisy. You know perfectly well that is not why you want those pearls. Don't try and bluff yourself, because it won't do."

The conversation turned to other topics. Jimmy was glad of it. He wanted to think this thing over.

From where he sat, he had an excellent view of the rope of pearls which was tugging him back to his old ways. And when he looked at them he could not see Molly. The thing was symbolical. It must be one or the other. He was at the crossroads. The affair was becoming a civil war. He felt like a rudderless boat between two currents. Eight years of gem collecting do not leave a man without a deep-rooted passion for the sport. As for that steel box, that was all nonsense. It was probably quite a good steel box, and the lock might very well be something out of the ordinary; but it could not be a harder job than some of those he had tackled.

The pearls shone in the lamplight. They seemed to be winking at him.

CHAPTER X

In a cozy corner of the electric flame department of the infernal regions there stands a little silver gridiron. It is the private property of his Satanic majesty, and is reserved exclusively for the man who invented amateur theatricals. It is hard to see why the amateur actor has been allowed to work his will unchecked for so long. These performances of his are diametrically opposed to the true sport of civilization, which insists that the good of the many should be considered as being of more importance than that of the few.

In the case of amateur theatricals, a large number of inoffensive people are annoyed simply in order that a mere handful of acquaintances may amuse themselves. Usually the whole thing can be laid at the door of the man, the organizer. He is the serpent in the Eden. Before his arrival, the house party were completely happy, and asked for nothing else but to be left alone. Then he arrives. At breakfast on his first morning, he strikes the first blow—casually helping himself to scrambled eggs the while, with the air of a man uttering some agreeable commonplace. "I say," he remarks, "why not get up some theatricals?" Eve, in the person of some young lady who would be a drawing-room reciter if drawing-room reciters were allowed nowadays, snatches at the apple. "Oh, yes," she says. "It ought to be for a charity," suggests somebody else. "Of course for a charity," says the serpent. Ten minutes later he has revealed the fact that he has brought down a little thing of his own which will just do, and is casting the parts. And after that the man who loves peace and quiet may as well pack up and

P. G. Wodehouse

leave. He will have no more rest in that house.

In the present case, the serpent was a volatile young gentleman of the name of Charteris. This indomitable person had the love of the stage ineradicably implanted in him. He wrote plays, and lived in hopes of seeing them staged at the leading theatres. Meanwhile, he was content to bring them out through the medium of amateur performances.

It says much for the basic excellence of this man's character that he was popular among his fellows, who, liking the man, overlooked the amateur stage manager.

The reign of unrest at the abbey was complete by the time Jimmy arrived there. The preliminary rehearsals had been gone through with by the company, who, being inexperienced, imagined the worst to be over.

Having hustled Jimmy into the vacant part, Charteris gave his energy free play. He conducted rehearsals with a vigor which occasionally almost welded the rabble which he was coaching into something approaching coherency. He never rested. He painted scenery, and left it about—wet—and people sat on it. He nailed up horseshoes for luck, and they fell on people. He distributed typed parts of the play among the company, and they lost them. But nothing daunted him.

"Mr. Charteris," said Lady Blunt after one somewhat energetic rehearsal, "is indefatigable. He whirled me about!"

This was perhaps his greatest triumph, that he had induced Lady Blunt to take part in the piece. Her first remark, on being asked, had been to the effect that she despised acting. Golden eloquence on the part of the author-manager had induced her to modify this opinion; and finally she had consented, on the understanding that she was not to be expected to attend every rehearsal, to play a small part.

The only drawback to an otherwise attractive scheme was the

fact that she would not be able to wear her jewels. Secretly, she would have given much to have done so; but the scene in which she was to appear was a daylight scene, in which the most expensive necklace would be out of place. So she had given up the idea with a stoicism that showed her to be of the stuff of which heroines are made.

These same jewels had ceased, after their first imperious call, to trouble Jimmy to the extent he had anticipated. It had been a bitter struggle during the first few days of his stay, but gradually he had fought the craving down, and now watched them across the dinner table at night with a calm which filled him with self-righteousness. On the other hand, he was uncomfortably alive to the fact that this triumph of his might be merely temporary. There the gems were, winking and beckoning to him across the table. At any moment—. When his thoughts arrived at this point, he would turn them—an effort was sometimes necessary—to Molly. Thinking of her, he forgot the pearls.

But the process of thinking of Molly was not one of unmixed comfort. A great uneasiness had gripped him. More than ever, as the days went by, he knew that he loved her, that now the old easy friendship was a mockery. But on her side he could see no signs that she desired a change in their relationship. She was still the old Molly of the New York days, frank, cheerful unembarrassed. But he found that in this new world of hers the opportunities of getting her to himself for any space of time were infinitesimal. It was her unfortunate conviction, bred of her American upbringing, that the duty of the hostess is to see that her guests enjoy themselves. Lady Jane held the English view that visitors like to be left to themselves. And Molly, noticing her stepmother's lack of enterprise and putting it down as merely another proof of her languid nature, had exerted herself all the more keenly to do the honors.

The consequence was that Jimmy found himself one of a crowd, and disliked the sensation.

The thing was becoming intolerable. Here was he, a young man in love, kept from proposing simply by a series of ridiculous obstacles. It could not go on. He must get her away somewhere by himself, not for a few minutes, as he had been doing up to the present, but for a solid space of time.

It was after a long and particularly irritating rehearsal that the idea of the lake suggested itself to him. The rehearsals took place in one of the upper rooms, and through the window, as he leaned gloomily against the wall, listening to a homily on the drama from Charteris, he could see the waters of the lake, lit up by the afternoon sun. It had been a terribly hot, oppressive day and there was thunder in the air. The rehearsal had bored everybody unspeakably. It would be heavenly on the lake, thought Jimmy. There was a Canadian canoe moored to that willow. If he could only get Molly.

"I'm awfully sorry, Jimmy," said Molly, as they walked out into the garden. "I should love to come. It would be too perfect. But I've half promised to play tennis."

"Who wants to play?"

"Mr. Wesson."

A correspondent of a London daily paper wrote to his editor not long ago to complain that there was a wave of profanity passing over the country. Jimmy added a silent but heartfelt contribution to that wave.

"Give him the slip," he said earnestly. It was the chance of a lifetime, a unique chance, perhaps his last chance, and it was to be lost for the sake of an ass like Wesson.

Molly looked doubtful.

"Well, come down to the water, and have a look at it," said Jimmy. "That'll be better than nothing."

They walked to the water's edge together in silence, Jimmy in a fever of anxiety. He looked behind him. No signs of Wesson yet. All might still be well.

"It does look nice, Jimmy, doesn't it?" said Molly, placing a foot on the side of the boat and rocking it gently.

"Come on," said Jimmy hoarsely. "Give him the slip. Get in."

Molly looked round hesitatingly.

"Well—oh, bother, there he is. And he's seen me."

Jimmy followed her gaze. The dapper figure of Mr. Wesson was moving down the lawn. He had a tennis racquet in his hand. His face wore an inviting smile.

Jimmy glared at him hopelessly.

Mr. Wesson had vanished now behind the great clamp of laurels which stood on the lowest terrace. In another moment he would reappear round them.

"Bother!" said Molly again. "Jimmy!" For gently, but with extreme firmness and dispatch, Jimmy, who ought to have known better, had seized her hand on the other side of the waist, swung her off her feet, and placed her carefully on the cushions in the bow of the canoe.

Then he had jumped in himself with a force which made the boat rock, and was now paddling with the silent energy of a dangerous lunatic into the middle of the lake; while Mr. Wesson, who had by this time rounded the laurels, stood transfixed, gazing glassily after the retreating vessel.

To the casual spectator, he might have seemed stricken dumb.

But at the end of the first ten seconds any fear that the casual spectator might have entertained as to the permanence of the seizure would have been relieved.

CHAPTER XI

"The man who lays a hand upon a woman," said Jimmy, paddling strongly, "save in the way of kindness—I'm very sorry, Molly, but you didn't seem able to make up your mind. You aren't angry, are you?"

There was a brief pause, while Molly apparently debated the matter in her mind.

"You wouldn't take me back even if I were angry," she said.

"You have guessed it," said Jimmy approvingly. "Do you read much poetry, Molly?"

"Why?"

"I was only thinking how neatly some of these poets put a thing. The chap who said, 'distance lends enchantment to the view,' for instance. Take the case of Wesson. He looks quite nice when you see him at a distance like this, with a good strip of water in between."

Mr. Wesson was still standing in a statuesque attitude on the bank. Molly, gazing over the side of the boat into the lake, abstained from feasting her eyes on the picturesque spectacle.

"Jolly the water looks," said Jimmy.

"I was just thinking it looked rather dirty."

P. G. Wodehouse

"Beastly," agreed Jimmy.

The water as a topic of conversation dried up. Mr. Wesson had started now to leave the stricken field. There was a reproachful look about his back which harassed Molly's sensitive conscience. Jimmy, on the other hand—men being of coarser fibre than women, especially as to the conscience—appeared in no way distressed at the sight.

"You oughtn't to have done it, Jimmy," said Molly.

"I had to. There seemed to be no other way of ever getting you by yourself for five minutes at a stretch. You're always in the middle of a crowd nowadays."

"But I must look after my guests."

"Not a bit of it. Let 'em rip. Why should they monopolize you?"

"It will be awfully unpleasant meeting Mr. Wesson after this."

"It is always unpleasant meeting Wesson."

"I shan't know what to say."

"Don't say anything."

"I shan't be able to look him in the face."

"That's a bit of luck for you."

"You aren't much help, Jimmy."

"The subject of Wesson doesn't inspire me somehow—I don't know why. Besides, you've simply got to say you changed your mind. You're a woman. It's expected of you."

"I feel awfully mean."

"What you want to do is to take your thoughts off the business. Keep your mind occupied with something else. Then you'll forget all about it. Keep talking to me about things. That's the plan. There are heaps of subjects. The weather, for instance, as a start. Hot, isn't it?"

"We're going to have a storm. There's a sort of feel in the air. We'd better go back, I think."

"Tush! And possibly bah!" said Jimmy, digging the paddle into the water. "We've only just started. I say, who was that man I saw you talking to after lunch?"

"How soon after lunch?"

"Just before the rehearsal. He was with your father. Short chap with a square face. Dressed in gray. I hadn't seen him before."

"Oh, that was Mr. Galer. A New York friend of father's."

"Did you know him out in New York?"

"I didn't. But he seems to know father very well."

"What's his name, did you say?"

"Galer. Samuel Galer. Did you ever hear of him?"

"Never. But there were several people in New York I didn't know. How did your father meet him over here?"

"He was stopping at the inn in the village, and he'd heard about the abbey being so old, so he came over to look at it, and the first person he met was father. He's going to stay in the house now. The cart was sent down for his things this afternoon. Did you feel a spot of rain then? I wish you'd paddle back."

"Not a drop. That storm's not coming till to-night. Why, it's a

　　　　　P. G. Wodehouse

gorgeous evening."

He turned the nose of the boat toward the island, which lay, cool and green and mysterious, in the middle of the lake. The heat was intense. The sun, as if conscious of having only a brief spell of work before it, blazed fiercely, with the apparent intention of showing what it could do before the rain came. The air felt curiously parched.

"There!" said Molly. "Surely you felt something, then."

"I did."

"Is there time to get back before it begins?"

"No."

"We shall get soaked!"

"Not a bit of it. On the other side of the island there is a handy little boat-house sort of place. We will put in there."

The boathouse was simply a little creek covered over with boards and capable of sheltering an ordinary rowing boat. Jimmy ran the canoe in just as the storm began, and turned her broadside on so that they could watch the rain, which was sweeping over the lake in sheets.

"Just in time," he said, shipping the paddle. "Snug in here, isn't it?"

"We *should* have got wet in another minute! I hope it won't last long."

"I hope it will, because I've got something very important to say to you, and I don't want to have to hurry it. Are you quite comfortable?"

"Yes, thanks."

"I don't know how to put it exactly. I mean, I don't want to offend you or anything. What I mean to say is—do you mind if I smoke? Thanks. I don't know why it is, but I always talk easier if I've got a cigarette going."

He rolled one with great deliberation and care. Molly watched him admiringly.

"You're the only man I've ever seen roll a cigarette properly, Jimmy," she said. "Everybody else leaves them all flabby at the ends."

"I learned the trick from a little Italian who kept a clothing store in the Bowery. It was the only useful thing he could do."

"Look at the rain!"

Jimmy leaned forward.

"Molly—"

"I wonder if poor Mr. Wesson got indoors before it began. I do hope he did."

Jimmy sat back again. He scowled. Every man is liable on occasion to behave like a sulky schoolboy. Jimmy did so.

"You seem to spend most of your time thinking about Wesson," he said savagely.

Molly had begun to hum a tune to herself as she watched the rain. She stopped. A profound and ghastly silence brooded over the canoe.

"Molly," said Jimmy at last, "I'm sorry."

No reply.

"Molly."

"Well?"

"I'm sorry."

Molly turned.

"I wish you wouldn't say things like that, Jimmy. It hurts—from you."

He could see that there were tears in her eyes.

"Molly, don't!"

She turned her head away once more.

"I can't help it, Jimmy. It hurts. Everything's so changed. I'm miserable. You wouldn't have said a thing like that in the old days."

"Molly, if you knew—"

"It's all right, Jimmy. It was silly of me. I'm all right now! The rain has stopped. Let's go back, shall we?"

"Not yet. For God's sake, not yet! This is my only chance. Directly we get back, it will be the same miserable business all over again; the same that it's been every day since I came to this place. Heavens! When you first told me that you were living at the abbey, I was absolutely happy, like a fool. I might have known how it would be. Every day there's a crowd round you. I never get a chance of talking to you. I consider myself lucky if you speak a couple of words to me. If I'd known the slow torture it was going to be, I'd have taken the next train back to London. I can't stand it. Molly, you remember what friends we were in the old days. Was it ever anything more with you? Was it? Is it now?"

"I was very fond of you, Jimmy." He could hardly hear the words.

"Was it ever anything more than that? Is it now? That was three years ago. You were a child. We were just good friends then. I don't want friendship now. It's not enough. I want you—*you*. You were right a moment ago. Everything *has* changed. For me, at least. Has it for you? Has it for you, Molly?"

On the island a thrush had begun to sing. Molly raised her head, as if to listen. The water lapped against the sides of the canoe.

"Has it, Molly?"

She bent over, and dabbled one finger in the water.

"I—I think it has, Jimmy," she whispered.

CHAPTER XII

The Honorable Louis Wesson, meanwhile, having left the water side, lit a cigarette, and proceeded to make a moody tour of the grounds. He felt aggrieved with the world. One is never at one's best and sunniest when a rival has performed a brilliant and successful piece of cutting-out work beneath one's very eyes. Something of a jaundiced tinge stains one's outlook on life in such circumstances. Mr. Wesson did not pretend to himself that he was violently in love with Molly. But he certainly admired her, and intended, unless he changed his mind later on, to marry her.

He walked, drawing thoughtfully at his cigarette. The more he reviewed the late episode, the less he liked it. He had not seen Jimmy put Molly in the canoe, and her departure seemed to him a deliberate desertion. She had promised to play tennis with him, and at the last moment she had gone off with this fellow Pitt. Who *was* Pitt? He was always in the way—shoving himself in.

At this moment, a large, warm raindrop fell on his hand. From the bushes all round came an ever-increasing patter. The sky was leaden.

He looked round him for shelter. He had reached the rose garden in the course of his perambulations. At the far end was a summerhouse. He turned up his coat collar and ran.

As he drew near, he heard a slow and dirgelike whistling

proceeding from the interior. Plunging in out of breath, just as the deluge began, he found Spennie seated at the little wooden table with an earnest expression on his face. The table was covered with cards.

"How Jim took exercise," said Spennie, glancing up. "Hello, Wesson. By Jove, isn't it coming down!"

With which greeting he turned his attention to his cards once more. He took one from the pack in his left hand, looked at it, hesitated for a moment, as if doubtful whereabouts on the table it would produce the most artistic effect; and finally put it down, face upward.

Then he moved another card from the table, and put it on top of the other one. Throughout the performance he whistled painfully.

Wesson regarded him with disfavor. "That looks damned exciting," he said. He reserved his more polished periods for use in public. "What are you playing at?"

"Wha-a-a'?" said Spennie abstractedly, dealing another card.

"Oh, don't sit there looking like a frog," said Wesson irritably. "*Talk*, man."

"What's the matter? What do you want? Hello, I've done it. No, I haven't. No luck at all. Haven't brought up a demon all day."

He gathered up the cards, and began to shuffle. "Ah, lov'," he sang sentimentally, with a vacant eye on the roof of the summerhouse, "could I bot tell thee how moch—"

"Oh, stop it!" said Wesson.

"You seem depressed, laddie. What's the matter? Ah, lov', could I bot tell thee—"

P. G. Wodehouse

"Spennie, who's this fellow Pitt?"

"Jimmy Pitt? Pal of mine. One of the absolute. Ay, nutty to the core, good my lord. Ah, lov', could I bot tell—"

"Where did you meet him?"

"London. Why?"

"He and your sister seem pretty good friends."

"I shouldn't wonder. Knew each other out in America. Bridge, bridge, ber-ridge, a capital game for two. Shuffle and cut and deal away, and let the lo-oser pay-ah. Ber-ridge—"

"Well, let's have a game, then. Anything for something to do. Curse this rain! We shall be cooped up here till dinner at this rate."

"Double dummy's a frightfully rotten game," said Spennie. "Ever played picquet? I could teach it to you in five minutes."

A look of almost awe came into Wesson's face, the look of one who sees a miracle performed before his eyes. For years he had been using all the large stock of diplomacy at his command to induce callow youths to play picquet with him and here was this admirable young man, this pearl among young men, positively offering to teach him. It was too much happiness. What had he done to deserve this? He felt as a toil-worn lion might have felt if an antelope, instead of making its customary bee line for the horizon, had expressed a friendly hope that it would be found tender and inserted its head between his jaws.

"I—it's very good of you. I shouldn't mind being shown the idea."

He listened attentively while Spennie explained at some length the principles which govern the game of picquet. Every now and then he asked a question. It was evident that he was beginning to grasp the idea of the game.

"*What* exactly is repicquing?" he asked, as Spennie paused.

"It's like this," said Spennie, returning to his lecture.

"Yes, I see now," said the neophyte.

They began playing. Spennie, as was only to be expected in a contest between teacher and student, won the first two hands. Wesson won the next.

"I've got the hang of it all right, now," he said complacently. "It's a simple sort of game. Make it more exciting, don't you think, if we played for something?"

"All right," said Spennie slowly, "if you like."

He would not have suggested it himself, but after all, hang it, if the man simply *asked* for it—It was not his fault if the winning of a hand should have given the fellow the impression that he knew all that there was to be known about picquet. Of course, picquet was a game where skill was practically bound to win. But—After all, Wesson had plenty of money. He could afford it.

"All right," said Spennie again. "How much?"

"Something fairly moderate. Ten bob a hundred?"

There is no doubt that Spennie ought at this suggestion to have corrected the novice's notion that ten shillings a hundred was fairly moderate. He knew that it was possible for a poor player to lose four hundred points in a twenty-minute game, and usual for him to lose two hundred. But he let the thing go.

"Very well," he said.

Twenty minutes later, Mr. Wesson was looking somewhat

ruefully at the score sheet. "I owe you eighteen shillings," he said. "Shall I pay you, now, or shall we settle up in a lump after we've finished?"

"What about stopping now?" said Spennie. "It's quite fine out."

"No, let's go on. I've nothing to do till dinner, and I'm sure you haven't."

Spennie's conscience made one last effort. "You'd much better stop, you know, Wesson, really," he said. "You can lose a frightful lot at this game."

"My dear Spennie," said Wesson stiffly, "I can look after myself, thanks. Of course, if you think you are risking too much, by all means—"

"Oh, if *you* don't mind," said Spennie, outraged, "I'm only too frightfully pleased. Only, remember I warned you."

"I'll bear it in mind. By the way, before we start, care to make it a sovereign a hundred?"

Spennie could not afford to play picquet for a sovereign a hundred, or anything like it; but after his adversary's innuendo it was impossible for a young gentleman of spirit to admit the humiliating fact. He nodded.

*   *   *   *   *

"It's about time, I fancy," said Mr. Wesson, looking at his watch an hour later, "that we were going in to dress for dinner."

Spennie made no reply. He was wrapped in thought.

"Let's see, that's twenty pounds you owe me, isn't it?" continued Mr. Wesson. "No hurry, of course. Any time you like. Shocking bad luck you had."

They went out into the rose garden.

"Jolly everything smells after the rain," said Mr. Wesson. "Freshened everything up."

Spennie did not appear to have noticed it. He seemed to be thinking of something else. His air was pensive and abstracted.

CHAPTER XIII

The emotions of a man who has just proposed and been accepted are complex and overwhelming. A certain stunned sensation is perhaps predominant. Blended with this is relief, the relief of a general who has brought a difficult campaign to a successful end, or of a member of a forlorn hope who finds that the danger is over, and he is still alive. To this must be added a newly born sense of magnificence, of finding oneself to be, without having known it, the devil of a fellow. We have dimly suspected, perhaps, from time to time that we were something rather out of the ordinary run of men, but there has always been a haunting fear that this view was to be attributed to a personal bias in our own favor. When, however, our suspicion is suddenly confirmed by the only judge for whose opinion we have the least respect, our bosom heaves with complacency, and the world has nothing more to offer.

With some accepted suitors there is an alloy of apprehension in the metal of their happiness; and the strain of an engagement sometimes brings with it even a faint shadow of regret. "She makes me buy new clothes," one swain, in the third quarter of his engagement, was overheard to moan to a friend. "Two new ties only yesterday." He seemed to be debating within himself whether human nature could stand the strain.

But, whatever tragedies may cloud the end of the period, its beginning at least is bathed in sunshine. Jimmy, regarding his lathered face in the glass as he dressed for dinner that night, called himself the luckiest man on earth, and wondered if he were worthy of such happiness. Thinking it over, he came to the conclusion that he was not, but that all the same he meant to have it.

No doubt distressed him. It might have occurred to him that the relations between Mr. McEachern and himself offered a very serious bar to his prospects; but in his present frame of mind he declined to consider the existence of the ex-constable at all. In a world that contained Molly there was no room for other people. They were not in the picture. They did not exist.

There are men in the world who, through long custom, can find themselves engaged without any particular whirl of emotion. King Solomon probably belonged to this class; and even Henry the Eighth must have become a trifle blasé in time. But to the average man, the novice, the fact of being accepted seems to divide existence into two definite parts, before and after. A sensitive conscience goads some into compiling a full and unexpurgated autobiography, the edition limited to one copy, which is presented to the lady most interested. Some men find a melancholy pleasure in these confessions. They like to draw the girl of their affections aside and have a long, cozy chat about what scoundrels they were before they met her.

But, after all, the past is past and cannot be altered, and it is to be supposed that, whatever we may have done in that checkered period, we intend to behave ourselves for the future. So, why harp on it?

Jimmy acted upon this plan. Many men in his place, no doubt, would have steered the conversation skillfully to the subject of the eighth commandment, and then said: "Talking about stealing, did I ever tell you that I was a burglar myself for about six years?" Jimmy was reticent. All that was over, he told himself. He had given it up. He had buried the past. Why exhume it? It did not occur to him to confess his New York crimes to Molly any more than to tell her that, when seven, he had been caned for stealing jam.

These things had happened to a man of the name of Jimmy Pitt, it was true. But it was not the Jimmy Pitt who had proposed to Molly in the canoe on the lake.

The vapid and irreflective reader may jump to the conclusion that Jimmy was a casuist, and ought to have been ashamed of himself.

He will be perfectly right.

On the other hand, one excuse may urged in his favor. His casuistry imposed upon himself.

To Jimmy, shaving, there entered, in the furtive manner habitual to that unreclaimed buccaneer, Spike Mullins.

"Say, Mr. Chames," he said.

"Well," said Jimmy, "and how goes the world with young Lord Fitz Mullins? Spike, have you ever been best man?"

"On your way! What's that?"

"Best man at a wedding. Chap who stands by the bridegroom with a hand on the scruff of his neck to see that he goes through with it. Fellow who looks after everything, crowds the crisp banknotes onto the clergyman after the ceremony, and then goes off and marries the first bridesmaid, and lives happily ever after."

"I ain't got no use for gettin' married, Mr. Chames."

"Spike, the misogynist! You wait, Spike. Some day love will awake in your heart, and you'll start writing poetry."

"I'se not dat kind of mug, Mr. Chames," protested Spike. "Dere *was* a goil, dough. Only I was never her steady. And she married one of de odder boys."

"Why didn't you knock him down and carry her off?"

"He was de lightweight champion of de woild."

"That makes a difference, doesn't it? But away with melancholy, Spike! I'm feeling as if somebody had given me Broadway for a birthday present."

"Youse to de good," agreed Spike.

"Well, any news? Keggs all right? How are you getting on?"

"Mr. Chames." Spike sank his voice to a whisper. "Dat's what I chased meself here about. Dere's a mug down in de soivant's hall what's a detective. Yes, dat's right, if I ever saw one."

"What makes you think so?"

"On your way, Mr. Chames! Can't I tell? I could pick out a fly cop out of a bunch of a thousand. Sure. Dis mug's vally to Sir Thomas, dat's him. But he ain't no vally. He's come to see dat no one don't get busy wit de jools. Say, what do you t'ink of dem jools, Mr. Chames?"

"Finest I ever saw."

"Yes, dat's right. De limit, ain't dey? Ain't youse really—"

"No, Spike, I am not, thank you *very* much for inquiring. I'm never going to touch a jewel again unless I've paid for it and got the receipt in my pocket."

Spike shuffled despondently.

"All the same," said Jimmy, "I shouldn't give yourself away to this detective. If he tries pumping you at all, give him the frozen face."

"Sure. But he ain't de only one."

P. G. Wodehouse

"What, *more* detectives? They'll have to put up 'house full' boards at this rate. Who's the other?"

"De mug what came dis afternoon. Ole man McEachern brought him. I seed Miss Molly talking to him."

"The chap from the inn? Why, that's an old New York friend of McEachern's."

"Anyhow, Mr. Chames, he's a sleut'. I can tell 'em by deir eyes and deir feet, and de whole of dem."

An idea came into Jimmy's mind.

"I see," he said. "Our friend McEachern has got him in to spy on us. I might have known he'd be up to something like that."

"Dat's right, Mr. Chames."

"Of course you may be mistaken."

"Not me, Mr. Chames."

"Anyhow, I shall be seeing him at dinner. I can get talking to him afterward. I shall soon find out what his game is."

For the moment, Molly was forgotten. The old reckless spirit was carrying him away. This thing was a deliberate challenge. He had been on parole. He had imagined that his word was all that McEachern had to rely on. But if the policeman had been working secretly against him all this time, his parole was withdrawn automatically. The thought that, if he did nothing, McEachern would put it down complacently to the vigilance of his detective and his own astuteness in engaging him stung Jimmy. His six years of burglary had given him an odd sort of professional pride. "I've half a mind," he said softly. The familiar expression on his face was not lost on Spike.

"To try for de jools, Mr. Chames?" he asked eagerly.

His words broke the spell. Molly resumed her place. The hard look died out of Jimmy's eyes.

"No," he said. "Not that. It can't be done."

"Yes, it could, Mr. Chames. Dead easy. I've been up to de room, and I've seen de box what de jools is put in at night. We could get at them easy as pullin' de plug out of a bottle. Say, dis is de softest proposition, dis house. Look what I got dis afternoon, Mr. Chames."

He plunged his hand into his pocket, and drew it out again. As he unclosed his fingers, Jimmy caught the gleam of precious stones.

He started as one who sees snakes in the grass.

"What the—" he gasped.

Spike was looking at his treasure-trove with an air of affectionate proprietorship.

"Where on earth did you get those?" asked Jimmy.

"Out of one of de rooms. Dey belonged to one of de loidies. It was de easiest old t'ing ever, Mr. Chames. I went in when dere was nobody about, and dere dey were on de toible. I never butted into anyt'ing so soft, Mr. Chames."

"Spike."

"Yes, Mr. Chames?"

"Do you remember the room you took them from?"

"Sure. It was de foist on de—"

"Then just listen to me for a moment. When we're at dinner, you've got to go to that room and put those things back—all

P. G. Wodehouse

of them, mind you—just where you found them. Do you understand?"

Spike's jaw had fallen.

"Put dem back, Mr. Chames!" he faltered.

"Every single one of them."

"Mr. Chames!" said Spike plaintively.

"You'll bear it in mind? Directly dinner has begun, every one of those things goes back where it belongs. See?"

"Very well, Mr. Chames."

The dejection in his voice would have moved the sternest to pity. Gloom had enveloped Spike's spirit. The sunlight had gone out of his life.

CHAPTER XIV

Spennie Blunt, meanwhile, was not feeling happy. Out of his life, too, had the sunshine gone. His assets amounted to one pound seven and fourpence and he owed twenty pounds. He had succeeded, after dinner, in borrowing five pounds from Jimmy, who was in the mood when he would have lent five pounds to anybody who asked for it, but beyond that he had had no successes in the course of a borrowing tour among the inmates of the abbey.

In the seclusion of his bedroom, he sat down to smoke a last cigarette and think the thing over in all its aspects. He could see no way out of his difficulties. The thought had something of the dull persistency of a toothache. It refused to leave him. If only this had happened at Oxford, he knew of twenty kindly men who would have rallied round him, and placed portions of their fathers' money at his disposal. But this was July. He would not see Oxford again for months. And, in the meantime, Wesson would be pressing for his money.

"Oh, damn!" he said.

He had come to this conclusion for the fiftieth time, when the door opened, and his creditor appeared in person. To Spennie, he looked like the embodiment of Fate, a sort of male Nemesis.

"I want to have a talk with you, Spennie," said Wesson, closing the door.

P. G. Wodehouse

"Well?"

Wesson lit a cigarette, and threw the match out of the window before replying.

"Look here, Spennie," he said, "I want to marry Miss McEachern."

Spennie was in no mood to listen to the love affairs of other men.

"Oh!" he said.

"Yes. And I want you to help me."

"Help you?"

"You must have a certain amount of influence with her. She's your sister."

"Stepsister."

"Same thing."

"Well, anyhow, it's no good coming to me. Nobody's likely to make Molly do a thing unless she wants to. I couldn't, if I tried for a year. We're good pals, and all that, but she'd shut me up like a knife if I went to her and said I wanted her to marry some one."

"Not being a perfect fool," said Wesson impatiently, "I don't suggest that you should do that."

"What's the idea, then?"

"You can easily talk about me to her. Praise me, and so on."

Spennie's eyes opened wide.

"Praise you? How?"

"Thanks," said Wesson, with a laugh. "If you can't think of any admirable qualities in me, you'd better invent some."

"I should feel such a silly ass."

"That would be a new experience for you, wouldn't it? And then you can arrange it so that I shall get chances of talking to her. You can bring us together."

Spennie's eyes became rounder.

"You seem to have mapped out quite a programme for me."

"She'll listen to you. You can help me a lot."

"Can I?"

Wesson threw away his cigarette.

"And there's another thing," he said. "You can queer that fellow Pitt's game. She's always with him now. You must get her away from him. Run him down to her. And get him out of this place as soon as possible. You invited him here. He doesn't expect to stop here indefinitely, I suppose? If you left, he'd have to, too. What you must do is to go back to London directly after the theatricals are over. He'll have to go with you. Then you can drop him in London and come back."

It is improbable that Wesson was blind to certain blemishes which could have been urged against this ingenious scheme by a critic with a nice sense of the honorable; but, in his general conduct of life, as in his play at cards, he was accustomed to ignore the rules when he felt disposed to do so. He proceeded to mention in detail a few of the things which he proposed to call upon his ally to do. A delicate pink flush might have been seen to spread over Spennie's face. He began to look like an angry rabbit. He had not a great deal of pride in his composition, but the thought of the ignominious role which Wesson was sketching out for him stirred what he had to its shallow depths.

Talking on, Wesson managed with his final words to add the last straw.

"Of course," he said, "that money you lost to me at picquet—What was it? Ten? Twenty? Twenty pounds, wasn't it? Well, we could look on that as canceled, of course. That will be all right."

Spennie exploded.

"Will it?" he cried, pink to the ears. "Will it, by George? I'll pay you every frightful penny of it before the end of the week. What do you take me for, I should like to know?"

"A fool, if you refuse my offer."

"I've a fearfully good mind to give you a most frightful kicking."

"I shouldn't try, Spennie, if I were you. It's not the form of indoor game at which you'd shine. Better stick to picquet."

"If you think I can't pay you your rotten money—"

"I do. But if you can, so much the better. Money is always useful."

"I may be a fool in some ways—"

"You understate it, my dear Spennie."

"But I'm not a cad."

"You're getting quite rosy, Spennie. Wrath is good for the complexion."

"And if you think you can bribe me to do your dirty work, you never made a bigger mistake in your life."

"Yes, I did," said Wesson, "when I thought you had some glimmerings of intelligence. But if it gives you any pleasure to behave like the juvenile lead in a melodrama, by all means do. Personally, I shouldn't have thought the game would be worth the candle. Your keen sense of honor, I understand you to say, will force you to pay your debt. It's an expensive luxury nowadays, Spennie. You mentioned the end of the week, I believe? That will suit me admirably. But if you change your mind, my offer is still open. Good night, Galahad."

CHAPTER XV

For pure discomfort there are few things in the world that can compete with the final rehearsals of an amateur theatrical performance at a country house. Every day the atmosphere becomes more and more heavily charged with restlessness and irritability. The producer of the piece, especially if he is also the author of it, develops a sort of intermittent insanity. He plucks at his mustache, if he has one; at his hair, if he has not. He mutters to himself. He gives vent to occasional despairing cries. The soothing suavity which marked his demeanor in the earlier rehearsals disappears. He no longer says with a winning smile: "Splendid, old man; splendid. Couldn't be better. But I think we'll take that over just once more, if you don't mind. You missed out a few rather good lines, and you forgot to give Miss Robinson her cue for upsetting the flowerpot." Instead, he rolls his eyes and snaps out: "Once more, please. This'll never do. At this rate we might just as well cut out the show altogether. For Heaven's sake, Brown, do try and remember your lines. It's no good having the best part in the piece if you go and forget everything you've got to say. What's that? All right on the night? No, it *won't* be all right on the night. And another thing. You *must* remember to say, 'How calm and peaceful the morning is', or how on earth do you think Miss Robinson is going to know when to upset that flowerpot? Now, then, once more; and do pull yourself together this time." After which the scene is sulkily resumed by the now thoroughly irritated actors; and conversation, when the parties concerned meet subsequently, is cold and strained.

Matters had reached this stage at the abbey. Everybody was thoroughly tired of the piece, and, but for the thought of the disappointment which—presumably—would rack the neighboring nobility and gentry if it were not to be produced, would have resigned without a twinge of regret. People who had schemed to get the best and longest parts were wishing now that they had been content with *First Footman* or *Giles, a villager.*

"I'll never run an amateur show again as long as I live," confided Charteris to Jimmy, almost tearfully the night before the production. "It's not good enough. Most of them aren't word-perfect yet. And we've just had the dress rehearsal!"

"It'll be all right on—"

"Oh, don't say it'll be all right on the night."

"I wasn't going to," said Jimmy. "I was going to say it'll be all right after the night. People will soon forget how badly the thing went."

"You're a nice, comforting sort of man, aren't you?" said Charteris.

"Why worry?" said Jimmy. "If you go on like this, it'll be Westminster Abbey for you in your prime. You'll be getting brain fever."

Jimmy himself was feeling particularly cheerful. He was deriving a keen amusement at present from the manoeuvres of Mr. Samuel Galer, of New York. This lynx-eyed man, having been instructed by Mr. McEachern to watch Jimmy, was doing so with a pertinacity which would have made a man with the snowiest of consciences suspicious. If Jimmy went to the billiard room after dinner, Mr. Galer was there to keep him company. If, during the course of the day, he had occasion to fetch a handkerchief or a cigarette case from his bedroom, he was sure, on emerging, to stumble upon Mr. Galer in the corridor. The employees of Wragge's Detective Agency, Ltd., believed in earning their salaries. Occasionally, after these encounters, Jimmy would come upon Sir Thomas Blunt's valet, the other man in whom Spike's trained eye had discerned the distinguishing trait of the detective. He was usually somewhere round the corner at these moments, and, when collided with, apologized with great politeness. It tickled Jimmy to think that both these giant brains should be so greatly exercised on his account.

Spennie, meanwhile, had been doing quite an unprecedented amount of thinking. Quite an intellectual pallor had begun to appear on his normally pink cheeks. He had discovered the profound truth that it is one thing to talk about paying one's debts, another actually to do it, and that this is more particularly the case when we owe twenty pounds and possess but six pounds seven shillings and fourpence. Spennie was acutely conscious of the fact that, if he could not follow up his words to Wesson with actual coin, the result would be something of an anticlimax. Somehow or other he would have to get the money—and at once. The difficulty was that no one seemed at all inclined to lend it to him.

There is a good deal to be said against stealing as a habit; but it cannot be denied that, in certain circumstances, it offers an admirable solution of a difficulty, and if the penalties were not so exceedingly unpleasant, it is probable that it would become far more fashionable than it is.

Spennie's mind did not turn immediately to this outlet from his embarrassment. He had never stolen before, and it did not occur to him directly to do so now. There is a conservative strain in all of us. But gradually, as it was borne in upon him that it was the only course possible, unless he applied to his stepfather—a task for which his courage was not sufficient—he found himself contemplating the possibility of having to secure the money by unlawful means. By lunch time, on the morning of the day fixed for the theatricals, he had decided definitely to do so. By dinner time he had fixed upon the object of his attentions.

With a vague idea of keeping the thing in the family, he had resolved to make his raid upon Sir Thomas Blunt. Somehow it did not seem so bad robbing one's relatives.

A man's first crime is, as a rule, a shockingly amateurish affair. Now and then, it is true, we find beginners forging with the accuracy of old hands or breaking into houses with the finish of experts. But these are isolated cases. The average tyro lacks generalship altogether. Spennie may be cited as a typical novice. It did not strike him that inquiries might be instituted by Sir Thomas, when he found his money gone, and that Wesson, finding a man whom he knew to be impecunious suddenly in possession of twenty pounds, might have suspicions. His mind was entirely filled with the thought of getting the money. There was no room in it for any other reflection.

His plan was simple. Sir Thomas, he knew, always carried a good deal of money with him. It was unlikely that he kept this on his person in the evening. A man to whom the set of his clothes is as important as it was to Sir Thomas, does not carry a pocket-book full of banknotes when he is dressed for dinner. He would leave it somewhere, reasoned Spennie. Where, he asked himself. The answer was easy. In his dressing room. Spennie's plan of campaign was complete.

The theatricals began at half-past eight. The audience had been hustled into their seats, happier than is usual in such circumstances from the rumor that the proceedings were to terminate with an informal dance. The abbey was singularly well constructed for such a purpose. There was plenty of room, and a sufficiency of retreat for those who sat out, in addition to a conservatory large enough to have married off half the couples in the county. The audience was in an excellent humor, and the monologue, the first item of the programme, was received with a warmth which gave Charteris, whom rehearsals had turned into a pessimist, a faint hope that the main item on the programme might not be the complete failure it had promised to be.

Spennie's idea had been to get through his burglarious specialty during the monologue, when his absence would not be noticed. It might be that if he disappeared later in the evening people would wonder what had become of him.

He lurked apart till the last of the audience had taken their seats. As he was passing through the hall, a hand fell on his shoulder. Conscience makes cowards of us all. Spennie bit his tongue and leaped three inches into the air.

"Hello, Charteris!" he said gaspingly.

"Spennie, my boyhood's only friend," said Charteris, "where are you off to?"

"What—what do you mean? I was just going upstairs."

"Then don't. You're wanted. Our prompter can't be found. I want you to take his place till he blows in. Come along."

The official prompter arrived at the end of the monologue with the remark that he had been having a bit of a smoke in the garden and his watch had gone wrong. Leaving him to discuss the point with Charteris, Spennie slipped quietly away, and flitted up the stairs toward Sir Thomas' dressing room. At the door, he stopped and listened. There was no sound. The house might have been deserted. He opened the door, and switched on the electric light.

Fortune was with him. On the dressing table, together with a bunch of keys and some small change, lay a brown leather pocketbook. Evidently Sir Thomas did not share Lady Blunt's impression that the world was waiting for a chance to rob him as soon as his back was turned.

Spennie opened the pocketbook, and counted the contents. There were two ten-pound notes, and four of five pounds.

He took a specimen of each variety, replaced the pocketbook, and crept out of the door.

Then he walked rapidly down the corridor to his own room.

Just as he reached it, he received a shock only less severe than the former one from the fact that this time no hand was placed on his shoulder.

"Spennie!" cried a voice.

He turned, to see Molly. She wore the costume of the stage milkmaid. Coming out of her room after dressing for her part, she had been in time to see Spennie emerge through Sir Thomas' door with a look on his face furtive enough to have made any jury bring in a verdict of guilty on any count without further evidence. She did not know what he had been doing; but she was very certain that it was something which he ought to have left undone.

"Er—hullo, Molly!" said Spennie bonelessly.

"What were you doing in Uncle Thomas' room, Spennie?"

"Nothing. I was just looking round."

"Just looking round?"

"That's all."

Molly was puzzled.

"Why did you look like that when you came out?"

"Like what?"

"So guilty."

"Guilty! What *are* you talking about?"

Molly suddenly saw light.

"Spennie," she said, "what were you putting in your pocket as you came out?"

"Putting in my pocket!" said Spennie, rallying with the desperation of one fighting a lost cause. "What do you mean?"

"You were putting something."

Another denial was hovering on Spennie's lips, when, in a flash, he saw what he had not seen before, the cloud of suspicion which must hang over him when the loss of the notes was discovered. Sir Thomas would remember that he had tried to borrow money from him. Wesson would wonder how he had become possessed of twenty pounds. And Molly had actually seen him coming out of the room, putting something in his pocket.

He threw himself at the mercy of the court.

"It's like this, Molly," he said. And, having prefaced his narrative with the sound remark that he had been a fool, he gave her a summary of recent events.

"I see," said Molly. "And you must pay him at once?"

"By the end of the week. We had—we had a bit of a row."

"What about?"

"Oh, nothing," said Spennie. "Anyhow, I told him I'd pay him by Saturday, and I don't want to have to climb down."

"Of course not. Jimmy shall lend you the money."

"Who? Jimmy Pitt?"

"Yes."

"But, I say, look here, Molly. I mean, I've been to him, already. He lent me a fiver. He might kick if I tried to touch him again so soon."

"I'll ask him for it."

"But, look here, Molly—"

"Jimmy and I are engaged, Spennie."

"What! Not really? I say, I'm frightfully pleased. He's one of the best. I'm fearfully glad. Why, that's absolutely topping. It'll be all right. I'll sweat to pay him back. I'll save out of my allowance. I can easily do it if I cut out a few things and don't go about so much. You're a frightfully good sort, Molly. I say, will you ask him to-night? I want to pay Wesson first thing to-morrow morning."

"Very well. You'd better give me those notes, Spennie. I'll put them back."

The amateur cracksman handed over his loot, and retired toward the stairs. Molly could hear him going down them three at a time, in a whirl of relief and good resolutions. She went to Sir Thomas' room, and replaced the notes. Having done this, she could not resist the temptation to examine herself in the glass for a few moments. Then she turned away, switched off the light, and was just about to leave the room when a soft footstep in the passage outside came to her ears.

She shrank back. She felt a curiously guilty sensation, as if she had been in the room with criminal rather than benevolent intentions. Her motives in being where she was were excellent—but she would wait till this person had passed before coming out into the passage.

Then it came to her with a shock that the person was not going to pass. The footsteps halted outside the door.

There was a curtain at her side, behind which hung certain suits of Sir Thomas'. She stepped noiselessly behind this.

The footsteps passed on into the room.

CHAPTER XVI

Jimmy had gone up to his room to put on the costume he was to wear in the first act at about the time when Spennie was being seized upon by Charteris to act as prompter. As he moved toward the stairs, a square-cut figure appeared.

It was the faithful Galer.

There was nothing in his appearance to betray the detective to the unskilled eye, but years of practice had left Spike with a sort of sixth sense as regarded the force. He could pierce the subtlest disguise. Jimmy had this gift in an almost equal degree, and it had not needed Mr. Galer's constant shadowing of himself to prove to Jimmy the correctness of Spike's judgment. He looked at the representative of Wragge's Detective Agency, Ltd., as he stood before him now, taking in his every detail: the square, unintelligent face; the badly cut clothes; the clumsy heels; the enormous feet.

"And this," he said to himself, "is the man McEachern thinks capable of tying my hands!" There were moments when the spectacle of Mr. Galer filled Jimmy with an odd sort of fury, a kind of hurt professional pride. The feeling that this espionage was a direct challenge enraged him. Behind this clumsy watcher he saw always the self-satisfied figure of Mr. McEachern. He seemed to hear him chuckling to himself.

"If it wasn't for Molly," he said to himself, "I'd teach McEachern a lesson. I'm trying to hold myself in, and he sets these fool detectives onto me. I shouldn't mind if he'd chosen somebody who knew the rudiments of the game, but Galer! Galer!

"Well, Mr. Galer," he said, aloud, "you aren't trying to escape, are you? You're coming in to see the show, aren't you?"

"Oh, yes," said the detective. "Jest wanted to go upstairs for 'alf a minute. You coming, too?"

"I was going to dress," said Jimmy, as they went up. "See you later," he added, at the door. "Hope you'll like the show."

He went into his room. Mr. Galer passed on.

*   *   *   *   *

Jimmy had finished dressing, and had picked up a book to occupy the ten minutes before he would be needed downstairs, when there burst into the room Spike Mullins, in a state of obvious excitement.

"Gee, Mr. Chames!"

"Hello, Spike."

Spike went to the door, opened it, and looked up and down the passage.

"Mr. Chames," he said, in a whisper, shutting the door, "there's bin doin's to-night for fair. Me coco's still buzzin'. Say, I was to Sir Thomas' dressin' room—"

"What! What were you doing there?"

Spike looked somewhat embarrassed. He grinned apologetically, and shuffled his feet.

"I've got dem, Mr. Chames," he said.

"Got them? Got what?"

"Dese."

He plunged his hand in his pocket, and drew forth a glittering mass. Jimmy's jaw dropped as he gazed at Lady Blunt's rope of pearls.

"Two hundred t'ousand plunks," murmured Spike, gazing lovingly at them. "I says to myself, Mr. Chames ain't got no time to be getting' after dem himself. He's too busy dese days wit' jollyin' along the swells. So it's up to me, I says, 'cos Mr. Chames'll be tickled to deat', all right, all right, if we can git away wit' dem. So I—"

Jimmy gave tongue with an energy which amazed his faithful follower.

"Spike! You lunatic! Didn't I tell you there was nothing doing when you wanted to take those things the other day?"

"Sure, Mr. Chames. But dose was little dinky t'ings. Dese poils is boids, for fair."

"Good heavens, Spike, you must be mad. Can't you see—Oh, Lord! Directly the loss of those pearls is discovered, we shall have those detectives after us in a minute. Didn't you know they had been watching us?"

An involuntary chuckle escaped Spike.

"'Scuse me, Mr. Chames, but dat's funny about dem sleut's. Listen. Dey's bin an' arrest each other."

"What!"

"Dat's right. Dey had a scrap in de dark, each finking de odder was after de jools, an' not knowin' dey was bote sleut's, an' now one of dem's bin an' taken de odder off, an' locked him in de cellar."

"What on earth do you mean?"

Spike giggled at the recollection.

"Listen, Mr. Chames, it's dis way. I'm in de dressin' room, chasin' around wit' dis lantern here for de jool box"—he produced from his other pocket a small bicycle lamp—"and just as I gets a line on it, gee! I hears a footstep comin' down de passage straight for de door. Was to de bad? Dat's right. Gee, I says to m'self, here's one of de sleut' guys what's bin an' got wise to me, and he's comin' in to put de grip on me. So I gets up, an' I blows out de lantern, and I stands dere in de dark, waitin' for him to come in. And den I'm going to get busy before he can see who I am, and jolt him one on de point, and den, while he's down and out, chase meself for de soivants' hall."

"Yes?" said Jimmy.

"Well, dis guy, he gets to de door, and opens it, and I'm just goin' to butt in, when dere suddenly jumps out from de room on de odder side de passage anodder guy, and gets de rapid strangleholt on dis foist mug. Say, wouldn't dat make you wonder was you on your feet or your coco?"

"Go on. What happened, then?"

"Dey begins to scrap good and hard in de dark. Dey couldn't see me, and I couldn't see dem, but I could hear dem bumpin' about an' sluggin' each odder, all right, all right. And by an' by one of dem puts de odder to de bad, so dat he goes down and takes de count; an' den I hears a click. And I know what dat is. One of de guys has put de irons on de odder guy. Den I hears him strike a light—I'd turned de switch what lights up de passage before I got into de room—and den he says, 'Ah', he says, 'got youse, have I? Not the boid I expected, but you'll do.' I knew his voice. It was dat mug what calls himself Galer."

"I suppose I'm the bird he expected," said Jimmy. "Well?"

"De odder mug was too busy catchin' up wit' his breat' to shoot it back swift, but after he's bin doin' de deep breathin' stunt for a while, he says, 'You mutt', he says, 'youse to de bad. You've made a break, you have.' He put it different, but dat's what he meant. Den he says that he's a sleut', too. Does de Galer mug give him de glad eye? Not on your life. He says dat dat's de woist tale that's ever bin handed to him. De odder mug says, 'I'm Sir Tummas' vally', he says. 'Aw, cut it out', says Galer. 'Sure youse ain't Sir Tummas himself?' 'Show me to him', says de foist guy, 'den you'll see.' 'Not on your life', says Galer. 'What! Butt in among de swells what's enjoyin' themselves and spoil deir evenin' by showin' dem a face like yours? To de woods! It's youse for de coal cellar, me man, and we'll see what youse has got to say afterward. G'wan!' And off dey went. And I lit me lantern again, got de jools, and chased meself here."

Jimmy stretched out his hand.

"All very exciting," he said. "And now you'll just hand me those pearls, and I'll seize the opportunity while the coast is clear to put them back where they belong."

Only for a moment did Spike hesitate. Then he pulled out the jewels, and placed them in Jimmy's hand. Mr. Chames was Mr. Chames, and what he said went. But his demeanor was tragic, telling eloquently of hopes blighted.

Jimmy took the necklace with a thrill. He was an expert in jewels, and a fine gem affected him much as a fine picture affects the artistic. He went to the light, and inspected them gloatingly.

As he did so, he uttered a surprised exclamation. He ran the jewels through his fingers. He scrutinized them again, more closely this time.

Then he turned to Spike, with a curious smile.

"You'd better be going downstairs," he said. "I'll just run along and replace them. Where is the box?"

"It's on de floor against de wall, near de window, Mr. Chames."

"Good. Better give me that lamp."

There was no one in the passage. He raced softly along it to Sir Thomas Blunt's dressing room.

He lit his lamp, and found the box without difficulty. Dropping the necklace in, he closed down the lid.

"They'll want a new lock, I'm afraid," he said. "However!"

He rose to his feet.

"Jimmy!" said a startled voice.

He whipped round. The light of the lamp fell on Molly, standing, pale and open-eyed, beside the curtain by the door.

CHAPTER XVII

Pressed, rigid, against the wall behind her curtain, Molly had listened in utter bewilderment to the sounds of strife in the passage outside. The half-heard conversation between the detectives had done nothing toward a solution of the mystery. Galer's voice she thought she recognized as one that she had heard before; but she could not identify it.

When the detectives had passed away together down the corridor, she had imagined that the adventure was at an end and that she was at liberty to emerge—cautiously—from her hiding place and follow them downstairs. She had stretched out a hand, to draw the curtain aside, when she caught sight of the yellow ray of the lamp on the floor, and shrank back again. As she did so, she heard the sound of breathing. Somebody was still in the room.

Her mystification deepened. She had supposed that the tale of visitors to the dressing room was complete with the two who had striven in the passage. Yet here was another.

She strained her ears to catch a sound. For a while she heard nothing. Then came a voice that she knew well; and, abandoning concealment, she came out into the room, and found Jimmy kneeling on the floor beside the rifled jewel box.

For a full minute they stood staring at each other, without a word. The light of the lamp hurt Molly's eyes. She put up a hand, to shade them. The silence was oppressive. It seemed to

P. G. Wodehouse

Molly that they had been standing like this for years.

Jimmy had not moved. There was something in his attitude which filled Molly with a vague fear. In the shadow behind the lamp, he looked shapeless and inhuman.

"What are you doing here?" he said at last, in a harsh, unnatural voice.

"I—"

She stopped.

"You're hurting my eyes," she said.

"I'm sorry. I didn't think. Is that better?"

He turned the light from her face. Something in his voice and the apologetic haste with which he moved the lamp seemed to relax the strain of the situation. The feeling of stunned surprise began to leave her. She found herself thinking coherently again.

The relief was but momentary. Why was Jimmy in the room at that time? Why had he a lamp? What had he been doing? The questions shot from her brain like sparks from an anvil.

The darkness began to tear at her nerves. She felt along the wall for the switch, and flooded the room with light.

Jimmy laid down the lantern, and stood for a moment, undecided. He looked at Molly, and suddenly there came over him an overwhelming desire to tell her everything. He had tried to stifle his conscience, to assure himself that the old days were over, and that there was no need to refer to them. And for a while he had imposed upon himself. But lately the falseness of his position had come home to him. He could not allow her to marry him, in ignorance of what he had been. It would be a villainous thing to do. Often he had tried to tell her, but had failed. He saw that it must be done, here and now.

He lifted the lid of the jewel box, and dangled the necklace before her eyes.

She drew back.

"Jimmy! You were—stealing them?"

"No, I was putting them back."

"Putting them back?"

"Listen. I'm going to tell you the truth, Molly—I've been trying to for days, but I never had the pluck. I wasn't stealing this necklace, but for seven years I lived by this sort of thing."

"By—"

"By stealing. By breaking into houses and stealing. There. It isn't nice, is it? But it's the truth. And whatever happens, I'm glad you know."

"Stealing!" said Molly slowly. "You!"

He took a step forward, and laid his hand on her arm. She shrank away from him. His hand fell to his side like lead.

"Molly, do you hate me?"

"How could you?" she whispered. "How could you?"

"Molly, I want to tell you a story. Are you listening? It's the story of a weak devil who was put up to fight the world, and wasn't strong enough for it. He got a bad start, and he never made it up. They sent him to school, the best school in the country; and he got expelled. Then they gave him a hundred pounds, and told him to make out for himself. He was seventeen, then. Seventeen, mind you. And all he knew was a little Latin and Greek, a very little, and nothing else. And they sent him out to make his fortune."

He stopped.

"It will be much simpler to tell it in the first person," he said, with a short laugh. "I arrived in New York—I was seventeen, you will remember—with ninety pounds in my pocket. It seemed illimitable wealth at the time. Two pounds was the most I had ever possessed before. I could not imagine its ever coming to an end. In dollars it seemed an inconceivable amount of money. I put up at the Waldorf. I remember, I took a cab there. I gave the man three dollars."

He laughed again.

"You can guess how long my ninety pounds lasted. Within a month I had begun to realize that my purse was shallower than I had thought. It occurred to me that work of some sort would be an advantage. I went round and tried to get some. My God! Remember, I was seventeen, and absolutely ignorant of every useful trade under the sun."

"Go on."

"One day I was lunching at the Quentin, when a man came and sat down at the same table, and we got into conversation. I had spent the morning answering want advertisements, and I was going to break my last twenty-dollar bill to pay for my lunch. I was in the frame of mind when I would have done anything, good or bad, that would have given me some money. The man was very friendly. After lunch, he took me off to his rooms. He had a couple of parlor rooms in Forty-fifth Street. Then he showed his hand. He was a pretty scoundrel, but I didn't care. I didn't care for anything, except that there seemed to be money to be had from him. Honesty! Put a man in New York with nineteen dollars and a few cents in his pockets, and no friends, and see what happens! It's a hell for the poor, in

New York. An iron, grinding city. It frightens you. It's so big and hard and cruel. It takes the fight out of you. I've felt it, and I know."

He stopped, and gave a little shiver. Nine years had passed since that day, but a man who has all but gone under in a big city does not readily forget the nightmare horror of it.

"Stone—that was the man's name—was running a tapless wire-tapping game. You've read about the trick, I expect. Every one has known about it since Larry Summerfield was sent to Sing Sing. But it was new then. There are lots of ways of doing it. Stone's was to hire a room and fix it up to look like a branch of the Western Union Telegraph Company. He would bring men in there and introduce them to a man he called the manager of the branch, who was supposed to get racing results ten minutes before they were sent out to the pool rooms. The victim would put up the money for a bet, and Stone and his friends got it at once. Stone was looking for an assistant. He wanted a man who looked like a gentleman. To inspire confidence! I looked older than I was, and he took me on. It was a filthy business, but I was in a panic. I was with Stone eight months. Then I left him. It was too unsavory—even for me.

"It was after that that I became a cracksman. I wanted money. It was no use hoping for work. I couldn't get it, and I couldn't have done it if I had got it. I was a pirate, and fit for nothing except piracy. One night I met a man in a Broadway rathskeller. I knew him by sight. I had seen him about at places. 'You're with Stone, aren't you?' he said, after we had talked about racing and other things for a while. I stared at him in surprise. I was frightened, too. 'It's all right', he said, 'I know all about Stone. You needn't be afraid of me. Aren't you with him?' 'I was', I said. 'You left him? Why?' I told him. 'You seem a bright kid', he said. 'Join me if you feel like it.' He was a cracksman. I never found out his real name. He was always called Bob. A curious man. He had been at Harvard, and spoke half a dozen languages. I think he took to burglary

P. G. Wodehouse

from sheer craving for excitement. He used to speak of it as if it were an art. I joined him, and he taught me all he knew. When he died—he was run over by a car—I went on with the thing. Then my uncle died, and I came back to England, rich.

"When I left the lawyer's office, I made up my mind that I would draw a line across my life. I swore I would never crack another crib. And when I met you I swore it again."

"And yet—"

"No. It isn't as bad as you think. When I was in London I fell in with a man named Mullins, who used to work with me in the old days. He was starving, so I took him in, and brought him along here with me, to keep him out of mischief. To-night he came to me with this necklace. He had been in here, and stolen it. I took it from him, and came to put it back. You believe me, don't you, Molly?"

"Yes," said she simply.

He came a step nearer.

"Molly, don't give me up. I know I've been a blackguard, but I swear that's all over now. I've drawn a line right through it. I oughtn't to have let myself love you. But I couldn't help it. I couldn't, dear. You won't give me up, will you? If you'd only take me in hand, you could make what you liked of me. I'd do anything for you. Any mortal thing you wanted. You can make me just anything you please. Will you try? Molly!"

He stopped. She held out both her hands to him.

The next moment she had gone.

CHAPTER XVIII

With a wonderful feeling of light-heartedness, Jimmy turned once more to the jewel box. He picked up the lamp and switched off the electric light. He had dropped the necklace to the floor, and had knelt to recover it when the opening of the door, followed by a blaze of light and a startled exclamation, brought him to his feet with a bound, blinking but alert.

In the doorway stood Sir Thomas Blunt. His face expressed the most lively astonishment. His bulging eyes were fixed upon the pearls in Jimmy's hand.

"Good evening," said Jimmy pleasantly.

Sir Thomas stammered. It is a disquieting experience to find the floor of one's dressing room occupied by a burglar.

"What—what—what—" said Sir Thomas.

"Out with it," said Jimmy.

"What—"

"I knew a man once who stammered," said Jimmy. "He used to chew dog biscuit while he was speaking. It cured him. Besides being nutritious."

"You—you blackguard!" said Sir Thomas.

P. G. Wodehouse

Jimmy placed the pearls carefully on the dressing table. Then he turned to Sir Thomas, with his hands in the pockets of his coat. It was a tight corner, but he had been in tighter in his time, and in this instance he fancied that he held a winning card. He found himself enjoying the interview.

"So—so it's you, is it?" said Sir Thomas.

"Who told you?"

"So you're a thief," went on the baronet viciously, "a low thief."

"Dash it all—I say, come now," protested Jimmy. "Not low. You may not know me, over here, but I've got a big American reputation. Ask anybody. But—

"And, I say," added Jimmy, "I know you don't mean to be offensive, but I wish you wouldn't call me a thief. I'm a cracksman. There's a world of difference between the two branches of the profession. I mean, well, suppose you were an actor-manager, you wouldn't like to be called a super, would you? I mean—well, you see don't you? An ordinary thief, for instance, would use violence in a case like this. Violence—except in extreme cases; I hope this won't be one of them—is contrary to cracksmen's etiquette. On the other hand, Sir Thomas, I should like to say that I have you covered."

There was a pipe in the pocket of his coat. He thrust the stem of this earnestly against the lining. Sir Thomas eyed the protuberance apprehensively, and turned a little pale.

"My gun, as you see, is in my pocket. It is loaded and cocked. It is pointing straight at you at the present moment, and my finger is on the trigger. I may add that I am a dead shot at a yard and a half. So I should recommend you *not* to touch that bell you are looking at."

Sir Thomas' hand wavered.

"Do, if you like, of course," said Jimmy agreeably. "In any case, I shan't fire to kill you. I shall just smash your knees. Beastly painful, but not fatal."

He waggled the pipe suggestively. Sir Thomas blanched. His hand fell to his side.

"How are the theatricals going?" asked Jimmy. "Did you like the monologue?"

Sir Thomas had backed away from the bell, but the retreat was merely for the convenience of the moment. He understood that it might be inconvenient to press the button just then; but he had recovered his composure by this time, and he saw that the game must be his. Jimmy was trapped, and he hastened to make this clear to him.

"How, may I ask," he said, "do you propose to leave the abbey?"

"I suppose they'll let me have the automobile," said Jimmy. "They can hardly ask me to walk. But I wasn't thinking of leaving just yet."

"You mean to stop!"

"Why not? It's a pretty place."

"And what steps, if I may ask, do you imagine I shall take?"

"Waltz steps. They're going to have a dance after the show, you know. You ought to be in that."

"You wish me, in fact, to become a silent accomplice? To refrain from mentioning this little matter?"

"You put things so well."

"And do you propose to keep my wife's jewels, or may I

P. G. Wodehouse

have them?"

"Oh, you may have those," said Jimmy.

"Thank you."

"I never touch paste."

Sir Thomas failed to see the significance of this remark. Jimmy repeated it, with emphasis.

"I never touch paste," he said, "and Lady Blunt's necklace is, I regret to say, made of that material."

Sir Thomas grew purple.

"Mind you," said Jimmy, "it's very good paste. I'll say that for it. I didn't see through it till I had it in my hands. Looking at the thing—even quite close—I was taken in for a moment."

The baronet made strange, gurgling noises.

"Paste!" he said, speaking with difficulty. "Paste! Paste! Damn your impertinence, sir! Are you aware that that necklace cost forty thousand pounds?"

"Then whoever paid that sum for it wasted a great deal of money. Paste it is, and paste it always will be."

"It can't be paste. How do you know?"

"How do I know? I'm an expert. Ask a jeweler how he knows diamonds from paste. He can feel them. He can almost smell them."

"Let me look. It's impossible."

"Certainly. I don't know the extent of your knowledge of pearls. If it is even moderate, I think you will admit that I am right."

Sir Thomas snatched the necklace from the table and darted with it to the electric light. He scrutinized it, breathing heavily. Jimmy's prophecy was fulfilled. The baronet burst into a vehement flood of oaths, and hurled the glittering mass across the room. The unemotional mask of the man seemed to have been torn off him. He shook with futile passion.

Jimmy watched him in interested silence.

Sir Thomas ran to the jewels, and would have crushed them beneath his feet, had not Jimmy sprang forward and jerked him away from them.

"Be quiet," he said. "Confound you, sir, will you stop that noise?"

Sir Thomas, unaccustomed to this style of address, checked the flood for a moment.

"Now," said Jimmy, "you see the situation. At present, you and I are the only persons alive, to the best of our knowledge, who know about this. Stay, though, there must be one other. The real necklace must have been stolen. It is impossible to say when. Years ago, perhaps. Well, that doesn't affect us. The thief, whoever he is, is not likely to reveal what he knows. So here you have it in a nutshell. Let me go, and don't say a word about having found me here, and I will do the same for you. No one will know that the necklace is not genuine. I shall not mention the subject, and I imagine that you will not. Very well, then. Now, for the alternative. Give me up, give the alarm, and I get—well, whatever they give me. I don't know what it would be, exactly. Something unpleasant. But what do you get out of it? Lady Blunt, if I may say so, is not precisely the sort of lady, I should think, who would bear a loss like this calmly. If I know her, she will shout loudly for another necklace, and see that she gets it. I should fancy you would find the expense unpleasantly heavy. That is only one disadvantage of the alternative. Others will suggest themselves to you. Which is it to be?"

Sir Thomas suspended his operation of glaring at the paste necklace to glare at Jimmy.

"Well?" said Jimmy. "I should like your decision as soon as it's convenient to you. They will be wanting me on the stage in a few minutes. Which is it to be?"

"Which?" snapped Sir Thomas. "Why, go away, and go to the devil!"

"All in good time," said Jimmy cheerfully. "I think you have chosen wisely. Coming downstairs?"

Sir Thomas made no response. He was regarding the necklace moodily.

"You'd better come. You'll enjoy the show. Charteris says it's the best piece there's been since 'The Magistrate'! And he ought to know. He wrote it. Well, good-by, then. See you downstairs later, I suppose?"

For some time after he had gone Sir Thomas stood, motionless. Then he went across the room and picked up the necklace. It occurred to him that if Lady Blunt found it lying in a corner, there would be questions. And questions from Lady Blunt ranked among the keenest of his trials.

* * * * *

"If I had gone into the army," said Jimmy complacently to himself, as he went downstairs, "I should have been a great general. Instead of which I go about the country, scoring off dyspeptic baronets. Well, well!"

CHAPTER XIX

The evening's entertainment was over. The last of the nobility and gentry had departed, and Mr. McEachern had retired to his lair to smoke—in his shirt sleeves—the last and best cigar of the day, when his solitude was invaded by his old New York friend, Mr. Samuel Galer.

"I've done a fair cop, sir," said Mr. Galer, without preamble, quivering with self-congratulation.

"How's that?" said the master of the house.

"A fair cop, sir. Caught him in the very blooming act, sir. Dark it was. Oo, pitch. Fair pitch. Like this, sir. Room opposite where the jewels was. One of the gents' bedrooms. Me hiding in there. Door on the jar. Waited a goodish bit. Footsteps. Hullo, they've stopped! Opened door a trifle and looked out. Couldn't see much. Just made out man's figure. Door of dressing room was open. Showed up against opening. Just see him. Caught you at it, my beauty, have I? says I to myself. Out I jumped. Got hold of him. Being a bit to the good in strength, and knowing something about the game, downed him after a while and got the darbies on him. Took him off and locked him in the cellar. That's how it *was*, sir."

"Good boy," said Mr. McEachern approvingly. "You're no rube."

"No, sir."

P. G. Wodehouse

"Put one of these cigars into your face."

"Thank you, sir. Very enjoyable thing, a cigar, sir. 'Specially a good un. I have a light, I thank you, sir."

"Well, and who was he?"

"Not the man you told me to watch, for. 'Nother chap altogether."

"That red-headed—"

"No, sir. Dark-haired chap. Seen him hanging about, suspicious, for a long time. Had my eye on him."

Mr. Galer chuckled reminiscently.

"Rummest card, sir, *I* ever lagged in my natural," he said.

"How's that? inquired Mr. McEachern amiably.

"Why," grinned Mr. Galer, "you'll hardly believe it, sir, but he had the impudence, the gall, if I may use the word, the sauce to tell me he was in my own line of business. A detective, sir! Said he was going into the room to keep guard. I said to him at the time, I said, it's too thin, cocky. That's to say—"

Mr. McEachern started.

"A detective!"

"A detective, sir," said Mr. Galer, with a chuckle. "I said to him at the time—"

"The valet!" cried Mr. McEachern.

"That's it, sir. Sir Thomas Blunt's valet, he was. That's how he got into the house, sir."

Mr. McEachern grunted despairingly.

"The man was right. He is a detective. Sir Thomas brought him down from London. He niver travels without him. Ye've done it. Ye've arristed wan of the bhoys."

Mr. Galer's jaw dropped slightly.

"He was? He really was—"

"Ye'd better go straight to where it was ye locked him up, and let him loose. And I'd suggest ye hand him an apology. G'wan, mister. Lively as you can step."

"I never thought—"

"That's the trouble with you fly cops," said his employer caustically. "Ye niver do think."

"It never occurred to me—"

"G'wan!" said the master of the house. "Up an alley!"

Mr. Galer departed.

"And I asked them," said Mr. McEachern, "I asked them particularly not to send me a rube!"

He lit another cigar, and began to brood over the folly of mankind.

He was in a very pessimistic frame of mind when Jimmy curveted into the room, with his head in the clouds and his feet on air.

"Can you spare me a few minutes, Mr. McEachern?" said Jimmy.

The policeman stared heavily.

P. G. Wodehouse

"I can," he said slowly. "What is ut?"

"Several things," said Jimmy, sitting down. "I'll take them in order. I'll start with our bright friend, Galer."

"Galer!"

"Of New York, according to you. Personally, I should think that he's seen about as much of New York as I have of Timbuctoo. Look here, McEachern, we've known each other some time, and I ask you, as man to man, do you think it playing the game to set a farmer like poor old Galer to watch me? I put it to you?"

The policeman stammered. The question chimed in so exactly with the opinion he had just formed, on his own account, of the human bloodhound who was now in the cellar making the peace with his injured fellow worker.

"Hits you where you live, that, doesn't it?" said Jimmy. "I wonder you didn't have more self-respect, let alone consideration for my feelings. I'm surprised at you."

"Ye're—"

"In fact, if you weren't going to be my father-in-law, I doubt if I could bring myself to forgive you. As it is, I overlook it."

The policeman's face turned purple.

"Only," said Jimmy, with quiet severity, taking a cigar from the box and snipping off the end, "don't let it occur again."

He lit the cigar. Mr. McEachern continued to stare fixedly at him. So might the colonel of a regiment have looked at the latest-joined subaltern, if the latter, during mess, had offered to teach him how to conduct himself on parade.

"I'm going to marry your daughter," said Jimmy.

"You are going to marry me daughter!" echoed Mr. McEachern, as one in a trance.

"I am going to marry your daughter."

The purple deepened on Mr. McEachern's face.

"More," said Jimmy, blowing a smoke ring. "*She* is going to marry me. We are going to marry each other," he explained.

McEachern's glare became frightful. He struggled for speech.

"I must congratulate you," said Jimmy, "on the way things went off tonight. It was a thorough success. Everybody was saying so. You're the most popular man in the county. What would they say of you at Jefferson Market, if they knew? By the way, do you correspond with any of the old set? Splendid fellows, they were. I wish we had some of them here tonight."

Mr. McEachern's emotions found relief in words. He rose, and waved a huge fist in Jimmy's face. His great body was shaking with rage.

"You!" shouted the policeman. "You!"

The fist was within an inch of Jimmy's chin.

Outwardly calm, inwardly very much alive to the fact that at any moment the primitive man in him might lead his prospective father-in-law beyond the confines of self-restraint, Jimmy sat still in his chair, his eyes fixed steadily on those of his relative-to-be. It was an uncomfortable moment. Mr. McEachern, if he made an assault, might regret it subsequently. But he would not be the first to do so. The man who did that would be a certain James Pitt. If it came to blows, the younger man could not hope to hold his own with the huge policeman.

"You!" roared McEachern. Jimmy fancied he could feel the

wind of moving fist. "You marry me daughter! A New York crook. The sweepings of the Bowery. A man who ought to be in jail. I'd like to break your face in."

"I noticed that," said Jimmy. "If it's all the same to you, will you take your fist out of my mouth? It makes it a little difficult to carry on a conversation. And I've several things I should like to say."

"Ye'll listen to me!"

"Certainly. You were saying?"

"Ye come here. Ye worm yourself into my house, crawl into it—"

"I came by invitation, and in passing, not on all fours. Mr. McEachern, may I ask one question?"

"What is ut?"

"If you didn't want me, why did you let me stop here?"

The policeman stopped as if he had received a blow. There came flooding back into his mind the recollection of his position. In his wrath, he had forgotten that Jimmy knew his secret. And he looked on Jimmy as a man who would use his knowledge.

He sat down heavily.

Jimmy went on smoking in silence for a while. He saw what was passing in his adversary's mind, and it seemed to him that it would do no harm to let the thing sink in.

"Look here, Mr. McEachern," he said, at last, "I wish you could listen quietly to me for a minute or two. There's really no reason on earth why we should always be at one another's throats in this way. We might just a well be friends, as we should be if we met now for the first time. Our difficulty is that we know too much about each other. You knew me in New York, and you know what I did there. Naturally, you don't like the idea of my marrying your daughter. You can't believe that I'm not simply an ordinary yegg, like the rest of the crooks you used to know. I promise you, I'm not. Can't you see that it doesn't matter what a man has been? It's what he is and what he means to be that counts. Mr. Patrick McEachern, of Corven Abbey, isn't the same as Constable McEachern, of the New York police. Well, then, I have nothing to do with the man I was when you knew me first. I have disowned him. He's a back number. I am an ordinary English gentleman now. My uncle has left me more than well off. I am a baronet. And is it likely that a baronet—*with* money, mind you—is going to carry on the yegg business as a side line? Be reasonable. There's really no possible objection to me now. Let's shake, and call the fight off. Does that go?"

The policeman was plainly not unmoved by these arguments. He drummed his fingers on the table, and stared thoughtfully at Jimmy.

"Is Molly—" he said, at length, "does Molly—"

"Yes," said Jimmy. "And I can promise you I love her. Come along, now. Why wait?"

McEachern looked doubtfully at Jimmy's outstretched hand. He moved his own an inch from the table, then let it fall again.

"Come on," said Jimmy. "Do it now. Be a sport."

And with a great grunt, which might have meant anything, from resignation to cordiality, Mr. McEachern capitulated.

P. G. Wodehouse

CHAPTER XX

The American liner, *St. Louis*, lay in the Empress Dock, at Southampton, taking aboard her passengers. All sorts and conditions of men flowed in an unceasing stream up the gangway.

Leaning over the second-class railing, Jimmy Pitt and Spike Mullins watched them thoughtfully.

Jimmy looked up at the Blue Peter that fluttered from the foremast, and then at Spike. The Bowery boy's face was stolid and expressionless. He was smoking a short wooden pipe, with an air of detachment.

"Well, Spike," said Jimmy. "Your schooner's on the tide now, isn't it? Your vessel's at the quay. You've got some queer-looking fellow travellers. Don't miss the two Cinghalese sports, and the man in the turban and the baggy breeches. I wonder if they're air-tight. Useful if he fell overboard."

"Sure," said Spike, directing a contemplative eye toward the garment in question. "He knows his business."

"I wonder what those men on the deck are writing. They've been scribbling away ever since we came here. Probably society journalists. We shall see in next week's *Sphere*: 'Among the second-class passengers we noticed Mr. "Spike" Mullins, looking as cheery as ever.' It's a pity you're so set on going, Spike. Why not change your mind, and stop?"

For a moment, Spike looked wistful. Then his countenance resumed its woodenness. "Dere ain't no use for me dis side, Mr. Chames," he said. "New York's de spot. Youse don't want none of me, now you're married. How's Miss Molly, Mr. Chames?"

"Splendid, Spike; thanks. We're going over to France by to-night's boat."

"It's been a queer business," said Jimmy, after a pause. "A deuced rum business. Well, I've come very well out of it, at any rate. It seems to me that you're the only one of us who doesn't end happily, Spike. I'm married. McEachern's butted into society so deep that it would take an excavating party with dynamite to get him out of it. Molly. Well, Molly's made a bad bargain, but I hope she won't regret it. We're all going some, except you. You're going out on the old trail again—which begins in Third Avenue and ends in Sing Sing. Why tear yourself away, Spike?"

Spike concentrated his gaze on a weedy young emigrant in a blue jersey, who was having his eye examined by the over-worked doctor, and seemed to be resenting it.

"Dere's nuttin' doin' dis side, Mr. Chames," he said, at length. "I want to get busy."

"Ulysses Mullins!" said Jimmy, looking at him curiously. "I know the feeling. There's only one cure, and I don't suppose you'll ever take it. You don't think a lot of women, do you? You're the rugged bachelor."

"Goils—" began Spike comprehensively, and abandoned the topic without dilating on it further.

Jimmy lit his pipe, and threw the match overboard. The sun came out from behind a cloud, and the water sparkled.

"Dose were great jools, Mr. Chames," said Spike thoughtfully.

"I believe you're still brooding over them, Spike."

"We could have got away wit' dem, if you'd have stood for it. Dead easy."

"You *are* brooding over them. Spike, I'll tell you something which will console you a little before you start out on your wanderings. That necklace was paste."

"What's dat?"

"Nothing but paste. They weren't worth thirty dollars."

A light of understanding came into Spike's eyes. His face beamed with the smile of one to whom dark matters are made clear.

"So *dat's* why you wouldn't stand for gettin' away wit' dem!" he exclaimed.

*   *   *   *   *

The last voyager had embarked. The deck was full to congestion.

"They'll be sending us ashore in a minute," said Jimmy. "I'd better be moving. Let me know how you're making out, Spike, from time to time. You know the address. And, I say. It's just possible you may find you want a dollar or two, every now and then. When you're going to buy another automobile, for instance. Well, you know where to write for it, don't you?"

"T'anks, Mr. Chames. But dat'll be all right. I'm going to sit in at another game dis time. Politics, Mr. Chames. A fr'en' of a mug what I knows has got a pull. Me brother Dan is an *alderman* wit' a grip on de 'Levent' Ward," he went on softly. "He'll find me a job!"

"You'll be a boss before you know where you are."

"Sure!" said Spike, grinning modestly.

"You ought to be a thundering success in American politics," said Jimmy. "You've got all the necessary qualities."

A steward passed.

"Any more for the shore?"

"Which shore?" asked Jimmy. "Well, Spike—"

"Good-by, Mr. Chames."

"Good-by," said Jimmy. "And good luck!"

* * * * *

Two tugs attached themselves excitedly to the liner's side. The great ship began to move slowly from the shore. Jimmy stood at the water side, and watched her. The rails were lined with gesticulating figures. In the front row, Spike waved his hat with silent vigor.

The sun had gone behind the clouds. As the ship slid out on its way, a stray beam pierced the grayness.

It shone on a red head.

ABOUT THE AUTHOR

 **Sir Pelham Grenville Wodehouse** KBE (October 15, 1881 – February 14, 1975) (pronounced WOOD-house) was an English comic writer who enjoyed enormous popular success for more than seventy years. Wodehouse was an acknowledged master of English prose admired both by contemporaries like Hilaire Belloc, Evelyn Waugh and Rudyard Kipling and by modern writers like Douglas Adams, Salman Rushdie, Terry Pratchett, and Stephen Fry. Sean O'Casey famously called him "English literature's performing flea", a derogatory description that Wodehouse cherished and adopted as the title of his autobiography. The Times has hailed him as a 'comic genius recognized in his lifetime as a classic and an old master of farce'.

Best known today for the Jeeves and Blandings Castle novels and short stories, Wodehouse was also a talented playwright and lyricist who was part author and writer of fifteen plays and of 250 lyrics for some thirty musical comedies. He worked with Cole Porter on the musical Anything Goes and frequently collaborated with Jerome Kern and Guy Bolton. He wrote the lyrics for the hit song "Bill" in Show Boat.

Choose from Thousands of 1stWorldLibrary Classics By

A. M. Barnard
Ada Leverson
Adolphus William Ward
Aesop
Agatha Christie
Alexander Aaronsohn
Alexander Kielland
Alexandre Dumas
Alfred Gatty
Alfred Ollivant
Alice Duer Miller
Alice Turner Curtis
Alice Dunbar
Allen Chapman
Alleyne Ireland
Ambrose Bierce
Amelia E. Barr
Amory H. Bradford
Andrew Lang
Andrew McFarland Davis
Andy Adams
Angela Brazil
Anna Alice Chapin
Anna Sewell
Annie Besant
Annie Hamilton Donnell
Annie Payson Call
Annie Roe Carr
Annonaymous
Anton Chekhov
Archibald Lee Fletcher
Arnold Bennett
Arthur C. Benson
Arthur Conan Doyle
Arthur M. Winfield
Arthur Ransome
Arthur Schnitzler
Arthur Train
Atticus
B.H. Baden-Powell
B. M. Bower
B. C. Chatterjee
Baroness Emmuska Orczy
Baroness Orczy
Basil King
Bayard Taylor
Ben Macomber
Bertha Muzzy Bower
Bjornstjerne Bjornson

Booth Tarkington
Boyd Cable
Bram Stoker
C. Collodi
C. E. Orr
C. M. Ingleby
Carolyn Wells
Catherine Parr Traill
Charles A. Eastman
Charles Amory Beach
Charles Dickens
Charles Dudley Warner
Charles Farrar Browne
Charles Ives
Charles Kingsley
Charles Klein
Charles Hanson Towne
Charles Lathrop Pack
Charles Romyn Dake
Charles Whibley
Charles Willing Beale
Charlotte M. Braeme
Charlotte M. Yonge
Charlotte Perkins Stetson
Clair W. Hayes
Clarence Day Jr.
Clarence E. Mulford
Clemence Housman
Confucius
Coningsby Dawson
Cornelis DeWitt Wilcox
Cyril Burleigh
D. H. Lawrence
Daniel Defoe
David Garnett
Dinah Craik
Don Carlos Janes
Donald Keyhoe
Dorothy Kilner
Dougan Clark
Douglas Fairbanks
E. Nesbit
E. P. Roe
E. Phillips Oppenheim
E. S. Brooks
Earl Barnes
Edgar Rice Burroughs
Edith Van Dyne
Edith Wharton

Edward Everett Hale
Edward J. O'Biren
Edward S. Ellis
Edwin L. Arnold
Eleanor Atkins
Eleanor Hallowell Abbott
Eliot Gregory
Elizabeth Gaskell
Elizabeth McCracken
Elizabeth Von Arnim
Ellem Key
Emerson Hough
Emilie F. Carlen
Emily Bronte
Emily Dickinson
Enid Bagnold
Enilor Macartney Lane
Erasmus W. Jones
Ernie Howard Pie
Ethel May Dell
Ethel Turner
Ethel Watts Mumford
Eugene Sue
Eugenie Foa
Eugene Wood
Eustace Hale Ball
Evelyn Everett-green
Everard Cotes
F. H. Cheley
F. J. Cross
F. Marion Crawford
Fannie E. Newberry
Federick Austin Ogg
Ferdinand Ossendowski
Fergus Hume
Florence A. Kilpatrick
Fremont B. Deering
Francis Bacon
Francis Darwin
Frances Hodgson Burnett
Frances Parkinson Keyes
Frank Gee Patchin
Frank Harris
Frank Jewett Mather
Frank L. Packard
Frank V. Webster
Frederic Stewart Isham
Frederick Trevor Hill
Frederick Winslow Taylor

Friedrich Kerst
Friedrich Nietzsche
Fyodor Dostoyevsky
G.A. Henty
G.K. Chesterton
Gabrielle E. Jackson
Garrett P. Serviss
Gaston Leroux
George A. Warren
George Ade
Geroge Bernard Shaw
George Cary Eggleston
George Durston
George Ebers
George Eliot
George Gissing
George MacDonald
George Meredith
George Orwell
George Sylvester Viereck
George Tucker
George W. Cable
George Wharton James
Gertrude Atherton
Gordon Casserly
Grace E. King
Grace Gallatin
Grace Greenwood
Grant Allen
Guillermo A. Sherwell
Gulielma Zollinger
Gustav Flaubert
H. A. Cody
H. B. Irving
H.C. Bailey
H. G. Wells
H. H. Munro
H. Irving Hancock
H. R. Naylor
H. Rider Haggard
H. W. C. Davis
Haldeman Julius
Hall Caine
Hamilton Wright Mabie
Hans Christian Andersen
Harold Avery
Harold McGrath
Harriet Beecher Stowe
Harry Castlemon
Harry Coghill
Harry Houidini

Hayden Carruth
Helent Hunt Jackson
Helen Nicolay
Hendrik Conscience
Hendy David Thoreau
Henri Barbusse
Henrik Ibsen
Henry Adams
Henry Ford
Henry Frost
Henry James
Henry Jones Ford
Henry Seton Merriman
Henry W Longfellow
Herbert A. Giles
Herbert Carter
Herbert N. Casson
Herman Hesse
Hildegard G. Frey
Homer
Honore De Balzac
Horace B. Day
Horace Walpole
Horatio Alger Jr.
Howard Pyle
Howard R. Garis
Hugh Lofting
Hugh Walpole
Humphry Ward
Ian Maclaren
Inez Haynes Gillmore
Irving Bacheller
Isabel Cecilia Williams
Isabel Hornibrook
Israel Abrahams
Ivan Turgenev
J.G.Austin
J. Henri Fabre
J. M. Barrie
J. M. Walsh
J. Macdonald Oxley
J. R. Miller
J. S. Fletcher
J. S. Knowles
J. Storer Clouston
J. W. Duffield
Jack London
Jacob Abbott
James Allen
James Andrews
James Baldwin

James Branch Cabell
James DeMille
James Joyce
James Lane Allen
James Lane Allen
James Oliver Curwood
James Oppenheim
James Otis
James R. Driscoll
Jane Abbott
Jane Austen
Jane L. Stewart
Janet Aldridge
Jens Peter Jacobsen
Jerome K. Jerome
Jessie Graham Flower
John Buchan
John Burroughs
John Cournos
John F. Kennedy
John Gay
John Glasworthy
John Habberton
John Joy Bell
John Kendrick Bangs
John Milton
John Philip Sousa
John Taintor Foote
Jonas Lauritz Idemil Lie
Jonathan Swift
Joseph A. Altsheler
Joseph Carey
Joseph Conrad
Joseph E. Badger Jr
Joseph Hergesheimer
Joseph Jacobs
Jules Vernes
Julian Hawthrone
Julie A Lippmann
Justin Huntly McCarthy
Kakuzo Okakura
Karle Wilson Baker
Kate Chopin
Kenneth Grahame
Kenneth McGaffey
Kate Langley Bosher
Kate Langley Bosher
Katherine Cecil Thurston
Katherine Stokes
L. A. Abbot
L. T. Meade

L. Frank Baum
Latta Griswold
Laura Dent Crane
Laura Lee Hope
Laurence Housman
Lawrence Beasley
Leo Tolstoy
Leonid Andreyev
Lewis Carroll
Lewis Sperry Chafer
Lilian Bell
Lloyd Osbourne
Louis Hughes
Louis Joseph Vance
Louis Tracy
Louisa May Alcott
Lucy Fitch Perkins
Lucy Maud Montgomery
Luther Benson
Lydia Miller Middleton
Lyndon Orr
M. Corvus
M. H. Adams
Margaret E. Sangster
Margret Howth
Margaret Vandercook
Margaret W. Hungerford
Margret Penrose
Maria Edgeworth
Maria Thompson Daviess
Mariano Azuela
Marion Polk Angellotti
Mark Overton
Mark Twain
Mary Austin
Mary Catherine Crowley
Mary Cole
Mary Hastings Bradley
Mary Roberts Rinehart
Mary Rowlandson
M. Wollstonecraft Shelley
Maud Lindsay
Max Beerbohm
Myra Kelly
Nathaniel Hawthrone
Nicolo Machiavelli
O. F. Walton
Oscar Wilde

Owen Johnson
P.G. Wodehouse
Paul and Mabel Thorne
Paul G. Tomlinson
Paul Severing
Percy Brebner
Percy Keese Fitzhugh
Peter B. Kyne
Plato
Quincy Allen
R. Derby Holmes
R. L. Stevenson
R. S. Ball
Rabindranath Tagore
Rahul Alvares
Ralph Bonehill
Ralph Henry Barbour
Ralph Victor
Ralph Waldo Emmerson
Rene Descartes
Ray Cummings
Rex Beach
Rex E. Beach
Richard Harding Davis
Richard Jefferies
Richard Le Gallienne
Robert Barr
Robert Frost
Robert Gordon Anderson
Robert L. Drake
Robert Lansing
Robert Lynd
Robert Michael Ballantyne
Robert W. Chambers
Rosa Nouchette Carey
Rudyard Kipling
Saint Augustine
Samuel B. Allison
Samuel Hopkins Adams
Sarah Bernhardt
Sarah C. Hallowell
Selma Lagerlof
Sherwood Anderson
Sigmund Freud
Standish O'Grady
Stanley Weyman
Stella Benson
Stella M. Francis

Stephen Crane
Stewart Edward White
Stijn Streuvels
Swami Abhedananda
Swami Parmananda
T. S. Ackland
T. S. Arthur
The Princess Der Ling
Thomas A. Janvier
Thomas A Kempis
Thomas Anderton
Thomas Bailey Aldrich
Thomas Bulfinch
Thomas De Quincey
Thomas Dixon
Thomas H. Huxley
Thomas Hardy
Thomas More
Thornton W. Burgess
U. S. Grant
Upton Sinclair
Valentine Williams
Various Authors
Vaughan Kester
Victor Appleton
Victor G. Durham
Victoria Cross
Virginia Woolf
Wadsworth Camp
Walter Camp
Walter Scott
Washington Irving
Wilbur Lawton
Wilkie Collins
Willa Cather
Willard F. Baker
William Dean Howells
William le Queux
W. Makepeace Thackeray
William W. Walter
William Shakespeare
Winston Churchill
Yei Theodora Ozaki
Yogi Ramacharaka
Young E. Allison
Zane Grey

www.ingramcontent.com/pod-product-compliance
Lightning Source LLC
Chambersburg PA
CBHW051843170626
46807CB00003B/1320